CW00864160

1,000,000 Books

are available to read at

www.ForgottenBooks.com

Read online
Download PDF
Purchase in print

ISBN 978-1-330-67776-6
PIBN 10091096

1 MONTH OF
FREE
READING

at

www.ForgottenBooks.com

By purchasing this book you are
eligible for one month membership to
ForgottenBooks.com, giving you
unlimited access to our entire
collection of over 1,000,000 titles via
our web site and mobile apps.

To claim your free month visit:

www.forgottenbooks.com/free91096

English
Français
Deutsche
Italiano
Español
Português

www.forgottenbooks.com

Mythology Photography **Fiction**
Fishing Christianity **Art** Cooking
Essays Buddhism Freemasonry
Medicine **Biology** Music **Ancient
Egypt** Evolution Carpentry Physics
Dance Geology **Mathematics** Fitness
Shakespeare **Folklore** Yoga Marketing
Confidence Immortality Biographies
Poetry **Psychology** Witchcraft
Electronics Chemistry History **Law**
Accounting **Philosophy** Anthropology
Alchemy Drama Quantum Mechanics
Atheism Sexual Health **Ancient History**
Entrepreneurship Languages Sport
Paleontology Needlework Islam
Metaphysics Investment Archaeology
Parenting Statistics Criminology
Motivational

m C

THE ROMANCE OF A PRISONER OF WAR IN THE REVOLUTION (SOUTH CAROLINA)

EDITED BY

JEFFERSON CARTER

Tyrteusque mihi nullo discrimine agetur

LONGMANS, GREEN AND CO.

FOURTH AVENUE & 30th STREET, NEW YORK
39 PATERNOSTER ROW, LONDON
BOMBAY, CALCUTTA, AND MADRAS
1919

tried and, failing, gave over......
against the saddle.'   p. 273

Madam Constantia

THE ROMANCE OF A PRISONER OF WAR IN THE REVOLUTION (SOUTH CAROLINA)

EDITED BY

JEFFERSON CARTER

Tros Tyriusque mihi nullo discrimine agetur

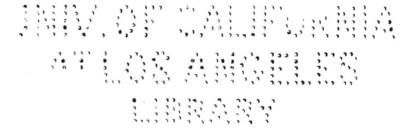

LONGMANS, GREEN AND CO.

FOURTH AVENUE & 30TH STREET, NEW YORK
39 PATERNOSTER ROW, LONDON
BOMBAY, CALCUTTA, AND MADRAS
1919

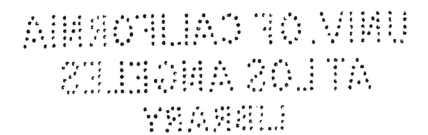

CONTENTS

EDITOR'S PREFACE

Although the Historical Manuscripts Commission (England) has dealt with several of the Northumberland Collections, the Commission has not thought fit to print among the papers of the Craven family of Osgodby, the narrative of the fifth baronet's experiences in South Carolina during the War of American Independence. The reason for this decision may be either a belief that the episode is not of value from a historical standpoint; or a suspicion that the facts owe something to the expansion of a man writing many years later. However this may be, the story seemed to the present Editor to possess a certain poignancy, and, notwithstanding some intimate passages, to be worthy of a public wider than that of the County of its birth. He has, therefore, with such skill as he possesses prepared it for publication.

It will be noticed that Sir Edward Craven nowhere names the regiment in which he served, but it appears from other sources that it was the 33rd Regiment of Foot, now styled the Duke of Wellington's Regiment.

The Editor has thought proper to retain the fanciful title prefixed by the writer, but has added some Chapter headings.

MADAM CONSTANTIA

CHAPTER I

SIR EDWARD'S PREFACE

So here is this fatal war commenced!
'The Child that is unborn shall rue
The hunting of that day!'

H. WALPOLE.

Not Lord Chatham, not Alexander the Great, nor Cæsar has
ever conquered so much territory in the course of all their wars
as Lord North has lost in one campaign!

C. J. FOX.

Six months ago I went through the old papers in the Strongroom. I noted that neither my father nor my grandfather had added a line, save in the way of leases and the like, to the records which the first and second baronets left of the Siege of Newcastle, and of the Union troubles. It occurred to me that we owed something to posterity; and that, for lack of more important matter, my fortunes *en campagne* in America were a part of the family history, and proper to be preserved.

For an idle man, however, to will and to do are two things; and I might never have proceeded beyond the former if I had not a day or two later taken up the Gentleman's Magazine and learned

that General Washington of the United States of
America had passed away at his seat at Mount
Vernon on the fourteenth of the preceding month.
That gave me the needed fillip. I never knew him;
at least I never knew him by that title, since on the
few occasions on which I met him, it was beyond
my duty as an officer in His Majesty's service to
admit the existence of the States. I believe him,
however, to have been a gentleman of good family,
kindly and dignified, somewhat of the old school,
and of considerable military ability; one, too, whose
influence went some way towards checking within
his sphere of action the rancour that in the Southern
Colonies stained the Continental Cause and did not
spare ours. Unfortunately from '80 onwards my
duty led me into the Carolinas; and it was to the
sad and unusual nature of the war in those provinces
that what was singular in my experiences was due.

Previously, to be brief, I had served for three
years in the north, I had suffered the humiliation
of surrendering with that gallant and loyal gentleman, General Burgoyne, I had been exchanged.
But my experiences in Canada and on the Hudson
were those of a hundred others and I pass over
them, proposing to begin my relation at the point at
which the fortunes of war cast me adrift, and flung
me on my own resources.

2

SIR EDWARD'S PREFACE

From where I write, looking out on the barren, frost-bound hills of the Border, it is a far cry to the rice-fields and tropical lands of the Tide-water of Carolina; and a farther cry to the rolling country of pleasant vale and forest that sweeps upwards to the foothills, and so to the misty distances of the Blue Ridge. In those days it was often a three months' passage, on salt meat and stale water; a passage of which many a poor fellow never saw the end. To-day I cross in a moment. But before I do so, let me add a word of preface, that all who read this may view the matter from our standpoint in '80, midway in the fighting, rather than from the point at which we stand to-day, with the end behind us and an American Minister at St. James's.

I say nothing about the Tea Duty or the claim to tax the Colonies. I believe that we had a right to have money from them; our fleet covered their trade. But whether we should not have left it to them to tax themselves is another matter, and seems more English. What is certain is, that we had through the war the most worthless government that ever held power in England; and so my father said a hundred times — and voted for them steadily till the day they fell!

In the City and at Brooks's the war was never popular. There were many in both who asked with

Mr. Walpole what we should gain by triumph itself; would America, laid waste, replace America
flourishing, rich and free? And here and there an
officer declined to serve against his kinsmen and was
allowed to stand aside. But for the most part we
ran to it, younger sons and eldest too, from my
neighbor Lord Percy downward, as to an adven-
ture. All who could beg or buy a commission
mounted the cockade. The thing was fashionable
— with two results that I came to think unhappy.

The first was that too many of our people —
those in particular who had the least right to do so
— looked down on the Colonials from a social height
as on a set of farmers and clodhoppers; forgetting
that many of them were our own cousins once or
twice removed, and that some had been bred up
beside us at Westminster and Oxford. The second
was that those of us who had seen service under the
great Frederick, or had learned our drill at Finchley
or Hounslow, sneered at the rebel officers as tailors,
called them Mohairs — God knows why! — and
made light not only of their skill but their courage,
treating even the Loyalists who joined us as of a
lower grade.

For these two prejudices we were to pay very
dearly. They not only brought into the struggle a
bitterness which was needless and to be deplored,

4

but, as things turned out, they reacted very unpleasantly on ourselves. It was bad enough to be worsted by those whom the meaner and more foolish among us regarded as of lower clay; it was still more mortifying for old soldiers, who had learned their drill in the barrack-yard, to find that it went for little in face of the immensities of that unknown continent; and that among the forests of the Hudson or in the marshes of the Savannah our military art was of far less value than the power to shoot straight, or to lay an ambush after the Indian fashion.

Owing to these two prejudices the lessons we had to learn in the war were the more painful. Not that our poor fellows did not fight. Believe me, they fought with the most dogged courage — sometimes when the only powder they had was the powder on their queues, and the steel or the clubbed musket was their only weapon. But the others fought too and stubbornly — what else could we expect? They were of our blood and bone; they, too, were Britons. And they were in their own forests, on their own rivers, — which seemed to be seas to us — they were fighting for their homes and barns and orchards. Whereas we were twelve weeks from home, ill-fed, ill-found, and ill-supported, scattered over hundreds of leagues, and lost in pathless wilds

5

that grew more hostile as outrage on the one side or the other embittered our relations.

The first half of the war was fought in the northern colonies. It ended sadly, as all remember, in our surrender at Saratoga, and in the retreat of General Clinton from Philadelphia to the sea-coast. After that, the fighting was transferred to the south, to Georgia, the Carolinas and Virginia. We took Charles Town, we defeated the Continental Army at Camden, we had South Carolina in our hands, we looked hopefully towards the north. And then, in the late summer of '80, when the south seemed to be in our hands, the country on all sides rose against us as by magic and the war took on a new and more savage character. But enough has been said by way of general preface.

For myself. On the fifth of October of that year '80, I was sent from Charlotte — whither my Lord Cornwallis had advanced on his way into North Carolina — with important orders to Colonel Ferguson, who at the time was covering the left flank with a strong body of royalists. On the sixth, accompanied by Simms, my orderly, and after a perilous ride, I reached Ferguson's camp on King's Mountain. He knew that the enemy were in strength in the neighbourhood, and, after falling back some distance, he had taken up a strong

position on a ridge, which rose above the forest —
a more active and able officer was not in the service.
But this time he had either under-valued his oppo-
nents, sturdy hunters and settlers from the Back-
waters, or he had over-estimated the strength of his
position; and the lamentable issue of the fight on
the following day is well known. After a fierce
struggle Ferguson's men were out-flanked and sur-
rounded, and he himself fell, striving bravely to the
last, while the greater part of his force was captured
or cut to pieces. Of the few who had the good
fortune to break through the ring I was one. Nor
was I only fortunate for myself, for I carried off
poor Simms on my crupper. From this point my
relation starts.

CHAPTER II

UNDER KING'S MOUNTAIN

But Major Ferguson by endeavoring to intercept the enemy in this retreat unfortunately gave time for fresh bodies of men to pass the mountains and to unite into a corps far superior to that which he commanded. They came up with him and after a sharp action entirely defeated him. Ferguson was killed and all his party either slain or taken.

RAWDON CORRESPONDENCE.

I was riding my grey, Minden, on that day, and I never wish to ride a better nag. But the weight of two heavy men is much for the staunchest horse, and when it fell, as it did a few yards short of safety, it came to the ground so heavily that the shock drove the breath out of my body. For a moment I did not know what had befallen me. I lay and felt nothing. If I thought at all, I supposed that the horse had stumbled. Then, coming to myself I tried to rise, and sank with the sweat starting from every pore.

Simms, three or four yards from me, lay still. The horse lay as still, but on my right shoulder, pinning me down and it needed no more to tell me that my sword-arm was broken, and that I was

8

helpless. The next thing that I remember, a man was standing some paces from me and covering me with one of their Deckhard rifles.

Instinct speaks before reason. "Don't shoot!" I cried.

"Why not?" he answered. "D — n you, your time is out! It was your turn at the Waxhaws and it's little quarter you gave us there! It's our turn to-day!"

Instinct prevailed once more. I knew that I could not rise, but I tried to rise. Then I fainted.]

When I opened my eyes again — to the circle of blue sky and the feathery tree-tops waving about the little clearing — the man was standing over me, a dark figure leaning on his gun. He was looking down at me. As soon as I could direct my mind to him, "You have the advantage of me, stranger," he said dryly. "A redcoat's no more to me than a quail. But shooting a man who shams to be dead is not in my way. It's you, that will pay the price, however."

"You'd not shoot a wounded man," I muttered — not that for the moment I seemed to care greatly.

"Who shot them at the Waxhaws?" he retorted savagely. "And hung them at Augusta? And gave them to the Indians to do worse things with? By G—d!" and with that he stopped speaking, and

9

with an ugly look, he handled his rifle as if he were going to knock out my brains with the stock.

But I was past fear and I was in pain. "Do your worst!" I said recklessly, "And God save the King!"

He lowered his gun and seemed to think better of it. He even smiled in an acrid sort of fashion, as he looked down at me. "Well, Britisher," he said, "you have the advantage of me! But if you can tell me what I am going to do with you —"

"Hospital," I murmured.

"Hospital!" he repeated. "Jerusalem! He says Hospital! Man, do you know that there are nine here who lost their folks at the Waxhaws, and thirty who are akin to them, and who've sworn, every man of them, to give no quarter to a Tory or an Englishman! And I'll not deny," he continued in a lower tone, "that I've sworn the same, and am perjured this moment. And he says — Hospital!"

"But the laws of war!" I protested weakly.

"Ay, you score them plainly enough on your poor devils' backs!"

"You make a mistake," I said. I was becoming a little clearer in my mind. "Those are the Articles of war."

"Indeed!" he replied. And he stared at me as if

10

he had never seen a King's officer before. Then "Why did you stop to pick up that fellow?" he asked, indicating poor Simms by a gesture. "If you'd ridden straight away, I should have been too late. It was your pause that gave me time to level at your horse and bring it down."

I raised myself on my elbow and found that the man had released me from Minden and had lifted me to the edge of the clearing. Simms still sprawled where he had fallen, with his arms cast wide and his neck awry. The horse lay half in and half out of the stagnant pool that lapped the roots of the trees on the farther side of the clearing.

"Is he dead?" I asked, staring at Simms.

"Neck broken," the man replied, "Who was he?"

"My orderly."

"Rank and file?"

"What else?" I said.

He grunted. "Is that in the Articles of War, too?" he said. "But any way, you did him little good, and wrecked yourself by it!" Then, in a different tone, "See here," he said, "you've tricked me, shamming to be dead and playing 'possum. I can't leave you to the buzzards, nor yet carry you to the camp, for they'll be for shooting you — shooting you, my friend, for certain! You'll have to ride if I can get you a horse. That is your only chance. I shall be away some time and if you wish to live you will lie close. It's not healthy anywhere this side of the Catawba for that uniform!"

I was in pain, but I was sufficiently myself to be anxious when he had left me; painfully anxious as time went on and he did not return. I lay staring at poor Simms; the flies were clustering on his face. I thought of the light heart with which I had ridden into Ferguson's camp and joined him and his volunteers the day before. I thought of the gay dinner we had eaten, and the toasts we had drunk, and the "Confusion to the Rebels" which we had planned — campaigning, a man learns to enjoy life as it comes. And then I thought of the day that had gone against us, miserably and unaccountably; of poor Ferguson, dragged and dead, with his foot in the stirrup and enough wounds in him to let out the lives of five men; of Husbands and Plummer and Martin — I had seen them all go down, — those, who had escaped in the fight, shot like rabbits in the last rush for the horses. By the laws of war, or of anything but this blind partisan fighting we should have won the battle against an equal number of undrilled farmers and backwoodsmen. We must have won. But we had lost; and I lay there under the sumach bushes that blended with the red of the old uniform; and if the man who had shot poor Minden at that last unlucky moment did not return, the buzzards would presently spy me out and Simms would not be the less fortunate of the two.

For the sounds of the fight had died away. The pursuit had taken another line, the silence of the forest was no longer torn by shot or scream. Even the excited chatter of the birds had ceased. The little clearing lay lonely, with the short twilight not far off — was that a buzzard already, that tiny speck in the sky?

What if the man did not come back?

But, thank God, even as I thought of this, I heard him. He came into view among the boles of the trees on the farther side of the clearing, riding one horse and leading another. He dismounted beside me and hooked the reins over a bough, and for the first time I took in what he was like. He appeared to be middle-aged, a tallish lean man, with hair that was turning gray. He wore a hunter's shirt and buckskin leggings, and with this, some show of uniform; a blue sash and a wide-brimmed hat with a white cockade were pretty well the sum of it. He had steely eyes — they showed light in the brown of his thin hard-bitten face. He stepped to the dead man and took from him a strap or two. Then he came to me.

"Now!" he said curtly. "Harden your heart,

13

King George! You'll wince once or twice before you are in that saddle. But when you are there you'll have a chance, and there's no other way you will have one! Now!"

To tell the truth, I winced already, having a horror of pain. But knowing that if I cried out, here was this rebel Yankee — who had no more nerves than a plantation Sambo — to hear me, I set my teeth while, with a splint made of two pieces of wood, he secured my arm in its due position, and eased as far as he could the crushed shoulder. He did it not untenderly, and when he rose to his feet, "You look pretty sick," he said, "as if you'd be the better for a sup of Kentucky whisky. But there's none here, and there's worse to come. So pull yourself together, and think of old England!"

He spoke in a tone of derision, to which the gentleness of his touch gave the lie. I rose to my feet and eyed the saddle. "It's that or the buzzards," he said, seeing that I hesitated; and he shoved me up. I did what I could myself and with an effort I climbed into the saddle. "That's good!" he exclaimed. "For a beginning."

I cried out once — I could not refrain; but I was mounted now if I could stay where I was. I suppose that he saw that I was on the verge of collapse, for "See here!" he cried roughly. "I can shoot you,

I can leave you, or I can take you. There is no other way. What do you say?"

"Go on," I said. And then, "Wait!"

"What now?" he growled, suspicious, I think, of my firmness.

"His address is on him," I said, nodding towards Simms. "He wanted his wife to know, if he did not come off. It's in his hat. I must take it."

He stared at me. For a moment I thought that he was going to refuse to do what I asked. Then he went and picked up Simms' hat and from a slit in the looped side he drew a thin packet of letters. "Are you satisfied now?" he said, as he handed the packet to me.

"That's it," I said. "Thank you."

"I thought you held that lot were only food for the triangles," he muttered. "Well, live and learn, and the last knows most! Now, forward it is, sir, and within five miles I'll have you under cover. All the same there's a plaguy bottom to cross that will give us trouble, or I am no prophet!"

I was soon to learn what he meant. For a certain distance, riding where it was level through open park-like land, that closed here and there into forest, the going was good and the pain was bearable, though the thought that at any moment the horse might stumble chilled me with apprehension. But

15

after a while we sank into a shallow valley, where the air was darkened by cypress trees and poisoned by their yew-like odor. And presently, threading the swamp that filled the bottom, there appeared a rivulet. It crossed our path, and my heart sank into my boots.

"Stay here," the man said shortly; and he left me and rode up and down, hunting for a crossing, while I followed him with scared eyes. At length he found what he wanted and he signed to me to join him. "Give me your rein," he said, "and hold on with all the strength you have! It's neck or nothing!"

We did it. But the muscles of the crushed shoulder and, in a less degree, the broken arm gave me exquisite pain, and I had to pause awhile on the other side of the water, crouching on the neck of my horse. When I had recovered, we went on and climbed out of the bottom and in another half mile as the light began to fail, we struck into a rough road.

We rode along it side by side, and he looked me over. "Major, ain't you?" he said by and by.

I admitted it.

"Only came in yesterday, did you?"

"That's so," I said. "How did you know?"

"Ah!" he said. "That's telling. But you may

take it from me, there's little we don't know. Ever been taken before, Major?"

In pain as I was I wondered what imp of mischief had suggested the question. "If you must know," I said reluctantly, "I was taken at Saratoga."

"And exchanged?"

"Yes," I said.

He chuckled. "Jerusalem!" he said. "You take it as easily as a snake takes skinning! Got a gift for it seemingly! But you escaped better last time than this, I guess?"

"Yes," I said grudgingly — why should I explain? And luckily at that moment a light showed a little way before us, and relieved me from farther questioning. The forest gave place to two or three ragged fields, divided by snake-fences; and beyond these, where our road crossed another, appeared a small log-house, backed by some straggling out-buildings. If appearances went for anything it was a tavern or a smithy. The light shone from a window of the house.

As we rode up to the door two or three dogs heard us and gave the alarm. The result was not promising. The light went out.

My companion swung his foot clear of the stirrup, and kicked the door. "House!" he cried. "House! Barter!"

There was no answer.

"House!" he cried again. "It's I! Wilmer!"

A window creaked. "Is that you, Captain?" a thin quavering voice asked.

"Who should it be?" my companion answered. "Don't be a fool! I want you."

A bar was removed — not very quickly — and the door was opened. By such firelight as issued from the room I saw an old man standing in the doorway, and behind him three or four white-faced women. He nursed a gun which he had barely the strength to level, and which he made haste to lower as soon as he had taken a look at us. "Lord-a-mercy, Cap'en, what a gunning there's been," he piped, peering up at us, all of a tremble. "We've been sweating here for hours, not knowing what moment the Tories and redcoats might be on us! Lord-a-mercy! Might ha' been the last day by the sound of it!"

"Father, let the Captain tell us," said one of the women.

"We've beaten them soundly," my companion answered with less blatancy than I expected. He seemed, indeed, to have two ways of talking, and to be by no means without education when he pleased to show it. "In a month or less," he continued, "there'll not be a red-coat this side of the

Santee High Hills; and if Marion does his work as well below, we shall be in Charles Town by Christmas! We shall have cleared Carolina, and you'll have no more need to sweat! But there, I want you to take in a wounded man, Barter. He's a broken arm, and a shoulder that, I expect, will give more trouble than the arm, and —"

"He's welcome!" the woman broke in heartily. "He's welcome to what we've got, Captain, and the Tories have left us! Let him come right in! Talking's poor fare, and —"

Her voice quavered away to nothing, she left the sentence unfinished. Before I had grasped what was amiss, or understood what was doing, the man and the women had crowded back into the house, the lower half of the door was closed, I heard a bolt shot. "No, no! you've no right to ask us!" the old man quavered. "You've no right to ask us, Cap'en! He's a redcoat! We'll take in no King's man and no Tory! Not we!"

"We daren't, Cap'en Wilmer," the woman said. "If we did the boys would take him out, and hang him, and, as likely as not, burn the house over us! It's as much as our lives are worth to take him in!"

"See here," the Captain answered, with more patience than I expected — it was clear that in spite of their refusal these people stood in awe of him. "See here! You can say that I put him here, Barter."

"And if you were here, it might do!" the woman replied. "May be so and may be not. But you're not here, Cap'en Wilmer, and when the boys' blood's up they'll not listen to father nor to me! We're a parcel of women, and you've no right to ask it. They've said, and you know it as well as I do, that they'll burn down any house that shelters a redcoat. We'll not take him!" she continued firmly, "and small kindness to him if we did! Phil Levi was here last Sunday and swore till he was black in the face what he'd do if we so much as fodder'd one of them! More by token, Cap'en, if you think it's safe — why do you not take him in at the Bluff?"

"It's a mile farther," Wilmer said, "and there are reasons."

"And we've reasons, too!" the woman retorted sharply. "I'd not lay a hand on him myself — God forbid I should — but I'll not shelter him. Jake is out with Colonel Marion below the Forks, and father hasn't strength to pull a trigger, and we're a parcel of women and 'tisn't fair to ask us! 'Tisn't fair to ask us, and we all alone!"

Wilmer swore softly. "D — n Phil Levi!" he said. "He's a brave fellow — before and after! But I can't say that I saw the color of his horse's tail to-day!" He sat forward in his saddle, under-termined, pondering.

I had borne up pretty well so far. Pride and the habit of a soldier's life had supported me under this man's scrutiny. I had told myself that it was the chance of war; that I was fortunate in being alive where so many — alas, so many! — who had sat at table with me a few hours before, had fallen. But, little by little, pain had sapped my fortitude. Every second in the saddle was a second of agony; every moment that my arm hung from the shoulder was a grinding pang. And on the threshold of this house, at the sound of the women's voices, I had thought that at last the worst was over. Here I had promised myself relief, rest, an end. The disappointment was the sharper. The refusal to take me in seemed to be fiendish, heartless, cruel. At the mere thought of it, of the barbarity of it, self-pity choked me, and I could have shed tears. "Let me be," I muttered. "I can bear no more."

"No, I'm d—d if I do," Wilmer answered angrily. "I had a reason for not taking you to my place, Major, but needs must when the devil drives, and it's there you are bound to go. We must make the best of it." He took my rein. "It's a long way to Salem," he continued, "but it's the last mile. Hold up! man, and maybe you'll see King George

21

yet. He certainly ought to be obliged to you,"
he added with a dry laugh. He kicked up his
horse.

I moved away with him, biting off the prayer
that rose to my lips that he would let me be. I
had no other thought now but to persist, to bear,
to keep the saddle; and the croak of the frogs, the
plaintive notes of the mocking bird in the thicket,
the change from clearing to forest and again from
forest to open fields — the open fields of a considerable plantation — all passed as the scenes pass
in a nightmare; now whelming me in despair,
as the blackness of the trees closed about us, now
lifting me to hope as lights broke out, twinkling
before us. Poor Ferguson, the fight, Simms, my
fall, all receded to an infinite distance; and only
one thing, only one thought, one aspiration remained — the craving to rest, to lie down, to come
to the end of pain. My shoulder was on fire; my
arm was red-hot iron. One moment I burned with
fever; the next I turned cold and faint and sick.

Only a mile! But from Newgate to Tyburn is
only a mile, yet how much lies between them for
the wretch condemned to suffer on the gallows.

At last I was aware that my companion had
alighted — perhaps he had done so more than once
— to pull down a sliprail. This time, whether it

was the last, or the only time, the rattle of the timber provoked an outburst of barking, and presently, amid the baying of dogs, a nigger's voice called out to know who was there. The alarm once given — and the hounds gave it pretty loudly — other voices joined in, in tones of alarm as well as joy. Lights glanced here and there; in a twinkling there were people about us. Black faces and white eye-balls appeared for an instant and sank into shadow. We halted before the porch of a long wooden house, that declared itself, here plainly and there dimly, as the lights fell upon it.

I could only endure. But surely the end was come now! Surely there would be rest for me here. They would come to me, they would do something for me presently.

Wilmer had gone up on the porch, and there was a woman — a woman in white with her arms about his neck. He was soothing her and she was laughing and crying at once; and about them and about me — who sat in the saddle below, in the dull lethargy of exhaustion — shone a ring of smiling, black faces. And then — here was something new, something startling and alarming — the woman was looking down at me, and speaking quickly and sharply; speaking almost as those other women had spoken at Barter's. She was pointing at me.

And the niggers were no longer laughing but staring, all staring at me. I gathered that they were frightened.

It could not be that there was no rest for me here? It could not be that they would not take me in here! Oh, it was impossible, it was inhuman, it was devilish! But I began to tremble. "Anywhere, anywhere but here!" the woman was saying. "It is madness to think of it. You know that, father! Why did you bring him here? When you knew! When you knew, father!"

"In the cabins, honey, if you like," the man answered patiently. "But he'll not be safe out of our sight."

She flared up. She poured out her anger upon him. "Safe!" she cried. "And what of you? Where will you be safe? And what is it to me if he be not safe? Don't do it, father, don't," she continued, her voice sinking to a note of entreaty. "Don't bring him here! It will end ill! You will see, it will end ill! Let him go to Barter's."

"We've been to Barter's —"

"And he won't take him! No! he's more sense, though the risk to him is small. But you, think how the day has gone, and left you safe and well! And now, now at the end, you will spoil all!'

"Let be, Con," the man struck in, speaking with decision. "He must come in. There's nothing else for it. We're not Cherokees, nor savages. There's nothing else that can be done. You must put up with it, and —"

In a twinkling she was at the foot of the steps and at my rein — a girl, young, slender, dark and fiercely excited. "If you are a man," she cried, seizing my arm, "if you are a gentleman, you'll not come here! Do you hear, sir! There are reasons, a thousand reasons why we cannot take you in. And more —"

On that word she stopped. A change came over her face as she looked into mine. The only answer I could give her — she had gripped my wounded arm and I could bear no more — was to faint away. As the man had said, I was in sore need of a sup of Kentucky whisky.

CHAPTER III

MADAM CONSTANTIA

I see how she doth wry,
When I begin to moan;
I see when I come nigh,
How fain she would be gone.

I see — what will ye more?
She will me gladly kill:
And you shall see therefore
That she shall have her will

ANON.

When I came to myself I was, by comparison, in a haven of comfort. I was in a clean bed, in a clean room, I was wearing a shirt that was also clean and was certainly not my own. A negro woman with a yellow kerchief bound about her head was holding a lamp, while a colored man who was bending over me, contrived a cage to lift the coverlet clear of my shoulder and arm. The room was small, with boarded walls, and the furniture was of plain wood and roughly made, of the kind that is found in the smaller plantations of this upper country. But my eye alighted on a framed sampler hung between two prints above the bedhead; and this and one or two handsome mahogany pieces

26

told a story of changes and journeys, which these, the cherished relics of an older house, perhaps in the Tidewater, had survived.

I noted these things dreamily, blissfully, resting in a haven of ease. Presently the man stood back to admire his work, and the woman, turning to glance at my face, saw that my eyes were open. She set down the lamp and fetching a cup held it to my lips. I have reason to believe that it held milk-punch; but for me it held nectar, and I drank greedily and as long as she would let me. Whatever it was, the draught cleared my mind; and when the man turned to the table and began to occupy himself with rolling up a monstrous length of bandage, I saw the woman sign to him. They looked towards the door, and I became aware of the voices of two people who were talking in an outer room. The speakers were the two who had debated my fate before, while I hung, worn out, over my horse's neck; and the question between them was apparently the same.

"But I can't see it, father!" the girl was saying, repeating it as if she had said it half a dozen times before. "I can't see it. What is he to us? Why should we do it? Think of my mother! Think of Dick! Haven't I heard you say a hundred times —"

"And a hundred to that! I admit it, Con," the man answered, "I have. But there was something about this fellow if you'll believe me —"

"About him!" she retorted, blazing up. "A weakling! A milksop! A poor thing who swoons under a minute's pain!"

"But if you had seen him pick the man up?" he pleaded. "It was that that took me, honey. It ran right athwart of all that I had heard of his like, and had seen of some of them! It was the devil of a mellay I can tell you! Of five who made off together after Ferguson was down he was the only one who fought his way through; and we were after him whip and spur. He was all but clear of us, when there came the other man running through the bush and calling to him, calling to him to take him up for God's sake! For God's sake! He stopped, Con! And I can tell you that to stop with the muzzles of our Deckhards between his shoulderblades and not forty yards off —"

"Who wouldn't have?" she retorted scornfully. "Is there a man that wouldn't have stopped? Is there a man who calls himself a man who could ride away —"

"Well, I fancy," he replied dryly, "I could put my hand on one or two, Con. I fancy I could."

"And because he did that," she continued stubbornly, "because he remembered, for just that one moment, that he and the men whom he hires to fight his battles were of the same flesh and blood as himself, you do this foolish, this mad, mad thing! To bring him here, father! To bring him to the Bluff of all places! Why, if it were only that I am alone — alone here —"

"There's Aunt Lyddy."

"And what is she? — it would be reason enough against it! But to be left here," the girl continued angrily — and it seemed to me that she was pacing the room — "alone for days together with this insolent Englishman who looks down on us, who calls us colonials and mohairs, and thinks us honored if he doesn't plunder us — and if he plunders us, what are we but rebels? Who will hardly stoop to be civil even to the men who are risking their all and betraying Carolina in his cause! Oh! it is too much!"

"He's not the worst of them at any rate," Wilmer replied with good humor. "Sit down, girl. And as to your being left with him, I don't know any one more able to take care of herself! If that be all —"

"But it's not all!" she cried. "It's not a quarter! If that were all I'd not say a word! But it's not that, you know it is not that!"

29

"I know it's not, honey!" he said in a different
tone — and I wondered to hear him, so gentle was
his voice. "I know it's not."

"If you were away altogether it would be different! If you kept away — "

"But I can't keep away," he answered mildly.
"I must come and go. I can't let the plantation
go to ruin. Times are bad enough and hard enough
— we may be burnt out any night. But until the
worst comes I must keep things together, Con, you
know that. It's fortunate that we're above King's
Mountain. After this Tarleton and his Greens —
d—n the fellow, I wish he had been there to-day
— will spread over the south side like a swarm of
wasps flocking to the honey-pot. But they'll be
shy of pushing as far north of Winsboro' as this
— we're too strong hereabouts. For the Englishman I'd send him to the cabins at once, but he
wouldn't be safe from our folks outside the house."

She spoke up suddenly. "If they come for him,"
she cried, "I warn you, father, I shall not raise a
finger to save him!"

"Pooh! pooh!"

"I vow I will not! So now you know!"

"Well, I don't think that they'll come," he replied lightly. "They know me, and —"

"To shelter a Britisher!"

"I've sheltered worse men," he responded reasonably.

"At least you've had warning!" she retorted — and I heard the legs of a chair grate on the floor of the outer room. "If I have to choose, your little finger is more to me than the lives of twenty such as he!"

"Unfortunately," he answered dryly, "it's not my little finger, my dear, that's in peril! It's my —"

"Father!" she cried, pain in her voice. "How can you! How can you!"

"There, there," he said, soothing her, "a man can but die once, and how he dies does not matter much! Courage, Con, courage, girl! Many is the awkward corner I have been in, as you know, and I've got out of it. You may be sure I shall take all the care I can."

"But you don't!" she retorted. "You don't! Or you would never let this man —" I lost the rest in the movement of a second chair.

For some minutes the two blacks had made hardly a pretence of attending to me. They had listened with all their ears. Once or twice when what was said had touched me nearly they had goggled their eyes at me between wonder and amazement. And I, too, wondered. I, too, saw that here was something that needed explanation. Why should this girl, scarcely out of her teens — I judged her to be no more that twenty — feel so strongly, so cruelly, so inhumanly? Why should she show herself so hard, so unnatural, where even her father betrayed the touch of nature that makes us all akin? This was a question, but it was one that I must consider to-morrow. For the present I was too comfortable, too drowsy, too weary. Sleep pressed on me irresistibly — the blessed sleep of the exhausted, of the wounded, of the broken, who are at last at rest! The room grew hazy, the light a dim halo. And yet before I slept I had a last impression of the things about me.

The girl came to the open door and stood on the threshold, gazing down at me. She was tall, slender, dark, and very handsome. She looked at me in silence for a long time, and with such a look and such a curiosity as one might turn on a crushed thing lying beside the road. It hurt me, but not for long.

For I slept, and dreamt of the Border and of home. I was in the small oak parlor at Osgodby. There was no fire on the hearth, it was summer and the bow-pots were full of roses. The windows were open, the garden, viewed through them, simmered in the sunshine.

My mother was sitting on the other side of the

empty hearth, fanning herself with a great yellow fan, and we were both looking at the picture of Henrietta Craven that is set in the overmantel. "Ill will come of it, ill will come of it," my mother was repeating over and over again. And then I found that it was not my mother who was saying it but the portrait over the fireplace; and — which did not seem to surprise me at the time — it was no longer the portrait of Henrietta Craven in her yellow sacque that spoke, but a woman in white, tall and slender and dark and very handsome.

. . . .

It was noon when I awoke; not the sultry noon of Charles Town, for the rains had come and the day was grey and cool. I was alone, in the pleasant stillness, but the door into the living room was ajar, perhaps that I might be heard if I called. Pigeons were cooing without, and not far away, probably on the veranda, some one was crooning in tune to the pleasant hum of a spinning-wheel. Sleep had made another man of me. My head was clear, I was free from fever, I was hungry; such pain as I felt was confined to the shoulder and arm. Yesterday I had come near to envying those who had fallen in the fight. To-day I was myself again, glad to be alive, free to hope, ready to look forward. After all, things might be worse; our Headquarters were at Charlotte,

barely thirty-five miles away, and if my Lord Cornwallis moved towards King's Mountain, to avenge
Ferguson, I might be rescued. If he did not, I
must contrive to be sent, as soon as I was well
enough to travel, to the rebel Headquarters in the
northern colony, whence I might be exchanged. I
should be safe there — I was not safe here. I must
see this man Wilmer by and by and talk to him about
it. He had shown a measure of humanity and some
generosity, mingled with his dry and saturnine
humor. And he had saved my life, I had no doubt
of that. In the meantime I was famished, positively
famished!

I called, "Hi! hi!"

The low crooning stopped, the hum of the spinning-wheel ceased. The negro woman who had held
the lamp appeared in the doorway. "How you
find yo'self dis mawning?" she asked. And then in
a lingo which at this distance of time I do not pretend to reproduce correctly, she asked me what I
would take to eat.

"There's nothing I could not eat," I said.

She showed her teeth in a wide smile. "Marse
mighty big man, dis mawning," she answered. "He
sorter lam-like yistiddy. He mo' like one er de
chilluns yistiddy. W'at you gwine ter eat?"

"Breakfast first!" I said. "Some tea, please —"

She shook her head violently. "Hole on **dar,**" she said. "I 'ear Ma'am Constantia say der ain't no tea fer Britishers! De last drap er dat **tea** bin gone sunk in Cooper River!"

"Oh!" I replied, a good deal taken aback. Confound Madam Constantia's impudence! "Then I will have what you will give me. Only let me have it soon."

"Marse mighty big man dis mawning," the woman said mischievously. "He'low he'll eat de last mossel der is. Yis'dy he mo' like one er de chilluns."

Well, I had the last morsel — without tea; while Mammy Jacks stood over me with her yellow kerchief and her good-natured grinning black face. "Who's Madam Constantia?" I asked after a time.

"W'at I tole you," the woman replied with dignity, "She, Ma'am Constantia ter cullud folks. She, missie ter me."

"The young lady I saw yesterday, is she?"

"Tooby sho'."

"She is Captain Wilmer's daughter, I suppose?"

"Dat's w'at I laid out fer to tell you."

I did not want to seem curious or I should have asked if "Madam" was married. I refrained out of prudence. I went on eating and Mammy Jacks went on looking at me, and presently, "I speck you monst'ous bad, cruel man," she said with unction. "I hear Ma'am Constantia say you make smart heap uv trubble fer cullud folks, en tote em to 'Badoes en Antigo! She say you drefful ar'ogant insolent Englishman! You too bad ter live, I' low."

"And Madam Constantia told you to tell me that?"

The woman's start and her look of alarm answered me. Before she could put in a protest, however, the negro who had been with her the previous evening appeared and relieved her from the difficulty. He came to attend to my arm, and did his work with a skill that would not have disgraced a passed surgeon. While he was going about the business, I was aware of a slender shadow on the threshold, the shadow of some one who listened, yet did not wish to be seen. "Confound her!" I thought. "The jade! I believe that she is there to hear me whimper!" And I set my teeth — she had called me a milksop, had she? — well, she should not hear me cry again. The shadow lay on the threshold a short minute, then it vanished. But more than once on that day and the two following days I was aware of it. It was all I saw of the girl; and though I knew, and had the best of grounds for knowing her sentiments respecting me, I confess that this steady avoidance of me — lonely and in pain as I was, and her guest — hurt me more than was reasonable.

As for Wilmer he was gone, without beat of drum, and without seeing me; and save Mammy Jacks and the nigger, Tom, no one came near me except Aunt Lyddy, and she came only once. She was a little old lady, deaf and smiling, who labored under the belief that I had met with my injuries in fighting against the French. She was quite unable to distinguish this war from the old French war; when she thought of the fighting at all, she thought of it as in progress in Canada or Louisiana, under the leadership of Braddock and Forbes and Wolfe. The taking of Quebec was to her an event of yesterday, and I might have drunk all the tea in the world, and she would not have objected. Such was Aunt Lyddy; and even, such as she was, I wondered with bitterness, that she was allowed to visit me.

Yet when I came to think more calmly, the position surprised me less. It was in the nature of this war to create a rancour which bred cruel deeds, and these again produced reprisals. After the capture of Charles Town in May and the subsequent defeat of Gates, the country had apparently returned to its allegiance. The King's friends had raised their heads. The waverers had declared themselves, opposition in the field had ceased. If one thing had seemed more certain than another it was that my Lord Cornwallis's base in the southern province was secure, and that he might now devote himself, without a backward glance, to the conquest of North Carolina and Virginia.

Then in a month, in a week, almost in a day had come a change. God knows whether it was the result of mismanagement on our part, or of some ill-judged severity; or, as many now think, of the lack of civil government, a lack ill-borne by a people of our race. At any rate the change came. In a week secret midnight war flamed up everywhere. In a month the whole province was on fire. Partisans came together and attacked their neighbors, rebels took loyalists by the throat, burned their houses, harried their plantations, and in turn suffered the same things. By day the King's writ ran; at first it was the exception for these irregulars to meet us in the field. But by night-attacks, by ambuscades, by besetting every ford and every ferry, they cut our communications, starved our posts and killed our messengers. For a time the royalists showed themselves as active. They, too, came together, formed bands, burned and harried. Presently the father was in one camp, the son in the other; neighbor fought with neighbor, old feuds were revived, old friendships were broken; and this it was that gave to this blind, bloody warfare, in the woods, in the morasses, in the cane-brakes, its savage character.

As quickly as General Gates's reputation had been lost, reputations were won. Marion, issuing from the swamps of the Pee Dee carried alarm to the gates of Charles Town. Sumter made his name a terror through all the country between the Broad and the Catawba Rivers. Colonel Campbell on the Watauga, Davy on the North Carolina border flung the fiery torch far and wide. It was all that Tarleton and his British Legion, the best force for this light work that we possessed, and Ferguson and his Provincials, now a shattered body — it was all that these could do to make head against the rebels or maintain the spirits of our party.

There were humane men, thank God, in both camps. But there were also men whom the memory of old wrongs wrought to madness. Cruel things were done. Quarter was refused, men were hung after capture, houses were burnt, women were made homeless. Therefore, no bitterness of feeling, no animosity, on one side or the other, was much of a surprise to me; rather I was prepared for it. But as the soldier by profession is the last, I, hope, to resort to these practices, so is he the most sorely hurt by them. And we, as I have said, had another grievance. Not only were we at a loss in this irregular fighting, but we had held our heads too high in the last war. We had looked down — the worst of us — on the Colonial officers. And now this was remembered against us. We were at once blamed and derided; our drill, our discipline, our service were turned to ridicule. - Nor was this shrew of a girl the first who had scoffed at our courage and made us the subject of her scorn.

Yet, though I understood her feelings, I was hurt. When a man is laid aside by illness or by an injury, something of the woman awakes in him, and he is wounded by trifles which would not touch him at another time. With Wilmer gone, with none but black faces about me, with no certainty of safety, I had only this girl to whom I could open my views or impart my wishes. And enemy as she was, she was a woman — in that lay much of my grievance. She was a woman, and the notion of the woman as his companion and comforter in sickness and pain is so deeply inbred in a man, that when she stands away from him at that time, it seems to him a thing monstrous and unnatural.

I think I felt her aloofness more keenly because, though I had barely seen her face, I was beginning to know her. The living-room, as in many of these

40

remote plantations, occupied the middle of the house, running through from front to rear. There was no second story and all the other chambers opened on this side or that of this middle room which served also for a passage. The business of the day was done in it, or on the veranda, according to the season. It followed that, though my door was now kept shut, I heard her voice a dozen, nay, a score of times a-day. In the morning I heard its full grave tones, mingling with the hurly-burly of business, giving orders, setting tasks, issuing laws to the plantation; later in the day I heard it lowered to the pitch of the afternoon stillness and the cooing of the innumerable pigeons that made the veranda their home.

I heard her most clearly when she raised her voice to speak to Aunt Lyddy; and aware that there is hardly a call upon the patience more trying than that made by deafness, I was surprised by the kindness and self-control of one who in my case had shown herself so hard and so inhuman.

"Confound her!" I thought more than once—the hours were long and dull, and I was often restless and in pain. "I wish I could see her, if it were only to rid myself of my impression of her. I don't suppose she is good-looking. I had only a glimpse of

her, and I was light-headed. When a man is in
that state every nurse is a Venus."

And then, on the fourth day, I did see her. I
heard some one approach my door and knock.
I thought that it was Mammy Jacks and I cried
"Come in!" But it was not Mammy Jacks. It was
Madam Constantia at last. She came in, and stood
a little within the doorway, looking down — not at
me but at my feet. And if she had not been all
that I had fancied her, and more, I might have had
eyes to read something of shame in her face, and
in the stiffness that did not deign to leave the threshold. She closed the door behind her. She closed
it with care it seemed to me.

"I cannot rise," I said, taking careful stock of
her, "honored as I am by your visit. Can I offer
you a chair, Miss Wilmer?"

"I do not need one," she replied. She was labor-
ing, I could see, under strong emotion, and was in
no mood for compliments. She was in white as I
had first seen her; and the quiet tones which I had
learned to associate with her, agreed perfectly with
the small head set on the neck as gracefully as a
lily on the stem, with the wide low brow, the serious
mouth, the firm chin. "I prefer to stand," she continued — and still she did not raise her eyes — I
wondered if they were black and hoped but could

hardly believe that they were blue. "I shall not keep you long, sir."

"You are not keeping me," I answered with irony. "I shall be here when you are gone, I fear, Miss Wilmer."

If I thought to work upon her feelings by that, and to force her to think of my loneliness, I failed wofully. "Not for long," she replied. "We are arranging to send you to Salisbury, sir. You will doubtless be sufficiently recovered to travel by to-morrow. You will be safer there than here, and will have better attendance in the hospital."

I was thunderstruck. "To-morrow!" I echoed. "Travel? But — but I could not!" I cried. "I could not, Miss Wilmer. The bones of my arm have not knit! You know what your roads are, and my shoulder is still painful, horribly painful."

"I am sorry, sir, that circumstances render it necessary."

"But, good heavens!" I cried, "You don't, you cannot mean it!"

"The man who put your arm in splints," she replied, averting her eyes from me, "will see that you are taken in a litter as far as the cross-roads. I have arranged for a cart to meet you there — a pallet and a —" her voice tailed off, I could not catch the last word. "They will see you carefully as far as —" again she muttered a name so low that I did not catch it — "on the way to Salisbury. Or to Hillsborough if that be necessary."

"Hillsborough?" I cried, aghast. "But have you reflected? It is eighty or ninety miles to Hillsborough! Ninety miles of rough roads — where there are roads, Madam!"

"It's not a matter of choice," she replied firmly — but I fancied that she turned a shade paler. "And it may not be necessary to go beyond Salisbury. At any rate the matter is settled, sir. Circumstances render it necessary."

"But it is impossible!" I urged. "It is out of the question!" The memory of my ride from King's Mountain, of the stream I had had to cross, was too sharp, too recent to permit me to entertain delusions. "The pain I suffered coming here —"

"Pain!" she cried, letting herself go at that. "What is a little pain, sir, in these days, when things so much worse, things unspeakable are being suffered — are being done and suffered every day? Our men whom you delivered to the Indians at Augusta, did they not suffer pain?"

"It was an abominable thing!" I said, aghast at her attitude. "But I did not do it, God forbid! I detest the thought of it, Miss Wilmer! And you, you do not mean that you would be as cruel as those —" I stopped. I let her imagine the rest. I held her with indignant eyes.

"I am doing the best I can," she said sullenly. But I saw that she was ashamed of her proposal even while she persisted in it; and I grew stronger in my resolve.

"I am helpless," I said. "Your father can do what he pleases, I am in his hands. But even he is bound by the laws of humanity, which he obeyed when he spared me. I cannot think that he did that, I cannot think that he behaved to me as one soldier to another in order to put me to torture! If he tells me I must go, I must go, I have no remedy. But until he does, I will never believe that it is his wish!"

"You will force yourself on us?" she cried, her voice quivering. "On us, two women as we are, and alone?"

I pointed to my shoulder. "I am not very dangerous," I said.

"I do not think you are, sir, or ever were," she retorted with venom. And now for the first time she met my look, her eyes sparkling with anger. "As one soldier to another!" she said. "It is marvellous that you should recognize him as a soldier! But I suppose that the habit of surrender is an education in many ways."

45

"Any one may insult a prisoner," I said. And I had the satisfaction of seeing the blood burn in her face. "But you did not come here to tell me that, Miss Wilmer."

"No," she answered. "I came here to tell you that you must go. You must go, sir."

"When your father sends me away," I said, "I must needs go. Until he does —"

"You will not?"

"No, Miss Wilmer, by your leave, I will not," I said with all the firmness of which I was capable. "Unless I am taken by force. And you are a woman. You will not be so untrue to yourself and to your sex as to use force to one, crippled as I am, and helpless as I am. Think! If your dogs broke a raccoon's leg, would you drag it a mile — two miles?"

The color ebbed from her face, and she shuddered — she who was proposing this! She shuddered at the picture of a brute's broken leg! And yet, strange to say, she clung to her purpose. She looked at me between anger and vexation, and "If I do not, others will," she said. "Do you understand that, sir? Is not that enough for you? Cannot you believe, cannot you do me the justice to believe that I am doing what I think to be right? That I am acting for the best? If you stay here

after this your blood be upon your own head!"
she added solemnly.

"So be it," I said. "It would be a very great
danger that would draw me from where I am, Miss
Wilmer. I am like the King of France, or whoever
it was, who said 'J'y suis, J'y reste.'"

"Stubborn! Foolish!" I heard her mutter.

"I hate pain," I said complacently.

"Do you hate pain more than you fear death?"
she asked, gazing at me with sombre eyes.

"I am afraid I do," I replied. "I am a milksop."
And I looked at her.

I was beginning to enjoy the discussion. But if
I hoped for a farther exchange of badinage with her
I was mistaken. She did not deign to reply. She
did that to which I could make no answer. She
went out and closed the door behind her.

CHAPTER IV

AT THE SMITHY

Hinc Constantia, illinc Furor.

CATULLUS.

The way in which the girl broke off the discussion and went out did more than surprise me. It left me anxious and, in a degree, apprehensive. Her proposal would have been a cruel and a heartless one if nothing lay behind it. If something lay behind it, some risk serious enough to justify the step on which she insisted, then I could think better of her but very much worse of my own plight.

Yet Wilmer had thought that I was safe in his house, if not in the huts. And if I were not secure here, what risks must I not run on the slow, painful, helpless journey to Gates's Head-Quarters, through a district ill-affected to the British! Once there, it is true, my life would be safe, and the Colonial Surgeons enjoyed a high reputation for skill. But the appliances of a rebel hospital were sure to be few, the fare rough and scanty; it was unlikely that I should be better off there than where I was. In the end, doubtless, I should have to go thither;

48

it was the only road to exchange and freedom, unless a happy chance rescued me. But a life which would be bearable when I could use my arm and had recovered my strength would be no bed of roses at present.

And to be quite honest I had found an interest where I was. I had enjoyed my tussle with this strange girl, and I looked forward to a repetition of it. Her beauty, her disdain, her desire to be rid of me piqued me — as whom would it not have piqued? — and whetted that appetite for conquest which is of the man, manly. Madam Constantia! The name suited her. I could fancy that she governed the plantation with a firm hand and a high courage.

On the whole I was determined, whatever the risk, to stay where I was; and yet as the day waned I felt less happy. My shoulder was painful, I was restless. I told myself that I had some fever. I was tired, too, of my own company and the house seemed more still than usual. I hoped that the girl would pay me another visit, would resume the argument, and make a second effort to persuade me; but she did not, and when my supper came Mammy Jacks dispensed it with an air, absurdly tragic. She heaved sighs from a capacious bosom, and looked at me as if I were already doomed.

"Marse, you'r runnin' up wid trubble," she said.

"Ma'am 'Stantia, she look like der wuz sump'n wrong. She look like she whip all de han's on de plantation."

"I dare say she is pretty severe," I said carelessly.

"I des'low you know nothin' 'bout it," the woman replied in great scorn. "She sholy not whip one ha'f, t'ree quarters, ten times 'nough! When Marse Wilmer come home, sez he, whip all dis black trash! Make up fer lost time. De last man better fer it! Begin wid Mammy Jacks! Dat's w'at he say, but I des hanker ter see him tech ole Mammy! I speck sumpin' wud happen bimeby ter 'sprise 'im. Ef Missie got win' uv it, she up en tell 'im!"

"Is he coming back soon?" I asked.

"Day atter tomorrow. Clar to goodness, when he mounts dem steps, Missie'll not mope round no mo'! She not make like she whip de han's den."

"She's very fond of him, is she?"

"Der ain't nobody in Car'lina fer 'er ceppin er dad! Seem like she idol — idol —"

"Idolizes him," I suggested.

"Mout be dat," Mammy Jacks assented. She repeated the word to herself with much satisfaction. It was a long one.

The little vixen, I thought. So she would be rid

of me before her father returned! She knew that he would not send me away, and so — well, she was a spit-fire!

"Look here, Mammy Jacks," I said. "I don't think that I shall sleep to-night. I am restless. I should like something to read. Will you ask Miss Wilmer if she can lend me a book. Any book will do, old or new."

"'Tooby sho,'" she said, and she went to do my bidding.

I thought that this might re-open relations. It might bring the girl herself to learn what kind of book I would choose to have. There was not likely to be much choice on this up-country plantation, where I need not expect to find the "Fool of Quality" or "The Female Quixote" or any of the fashionable productions of the circulating libraries. But a Pope, a Richardson, or possibly a Fielding I might hope to have.

Alas, my reckoning was at fault. I had none of these. It was Mammy Jacks who presently brought back the answer and the book. "Missie, she up 'n say dat monst'ous good book fer you," the negress explained, as she set down the volume with a grin. "Missie say it wuz ole en new, but she specks new ter you. She tuck'n say she 'ope you read it ter night — you in monst'ous big need uv it."

Puzzled by the message, and a little curious, I took the book and opened it. It was the Bible!

For a moment I was very angry; it seemed to be a poor jest, and in bad taste. Then I saw, or thought that I saw, that it was not a jest at all. This queer girl had sent the Bible, thinking to impress me, to frighten me, to bend me at the last moment to her will!

Certainly she should not persuade me now! Go? Never!

After all I had a quiet night. I slept well and awoke with a keen desire to turn the tables on her. I counted on her coming to learn the result of her last step, perhaps to try the effect of a last persuasion. But she did not come near me, and the day passed very slowly. I thanked heaven that Wilmer would return on the morrow. I should have some one to speak to then, some one to look at, I should no longer be cut off from my kind. And he might bring news, news of Tarleton, news of Lord Cornwallis, news of our movements in the field. Out of pure ennui I dozed through most of the afternoon. The sun set and the short twilight passed unnoticed. It was dark when I awoke. I wondered for a moment where I was. Then I remembered, and fancied that I must have slept some hours, for I was hungry.

And then, "Wilmer has come," I thought; I heard the voice of a man in the living-room. Presently I heard another voice, nay, more than one. "Yes, Wilmer has come," I thought, "and not alone. I shall have some one to speak to at last, and news perhaps. Doubtless they are occupied with him, but they need not forget me altogether. They might bring me a light and my supper."

And then — strange how swiftly, in a flash, in a heartbeat, the mind seizes and accepts a new state of things! — then I knew why Mammy Jacks had brought no light and no supper. I heard her voice, excited, tearful, protesting, raised in the unrestrained vehemence of the black; and a man's voice that silenced her harshly, silenced her with an oath. And therewith I needed no more to explain the position. I grasped it.

When a few seconds later the door was flung open, and the light broke in upon me, and with the light three or four rough burly figures, who crowded one after the other over the threshold, I was prepared. I had had that moment of warning, and I was ready. There were scared black faces behind them, filling the doorway, and peeping athwart them, and murmurs, and a stir of panic proceeding from the room without.

"You come without much ceremony, gentlemen,"

53

I said, speaking as coolly as I could. For the moment I had only one thought, one aim, one anxiety — that what I felt should not appear.

"Ceremony? Oh, d—n your ceremony!" cried the first to enter. And he called for a candle that he might see what he was doing. When it was handed in I saw them. They were a grim, rough group, the man who had called for the candle the least ill-looking among them; as he was also the smallest and perhaps the most dangerous. They all wore wide-leafed hats and carried guns and were hung about with pouches and weapons. They stared down at me, and I stared steadily at them. "You've got to swap your bed for the road," the leader continued in the same brutal tone. "We think you'll be safer, where we're going to take you, mister."

"And where's that?" I asked — though I knew very well.

"To Salisbury," he said. But his grin gave the lie to his words.

"I am afraid that is too long a journey, gentlemen," I answered. "I could not go so far. I am quite helpless."

"Oh, you'll be helped to make the journey," he retorted; and they all laughed, as at a good jest. "You'll not find it long, either," he continued, "you can trust us for that. We're not set on long journeys ourselves. We must go with you a piece of the way, so we'll shorten it, depend upon it!"

"I am Captain Wilmer's prisoner," I said clutching at what I knew was a straw. "He placed me here, and you will have to answer to him, gentlemen, for anything you may do."

"We'll answer him," growled one of the other men. "I don't think you'll be there to complain," he added with meaning.

I tried to calculate the chances, but there were none. I could not resist, I was crippled and unarmed. I could not escape. I was in their hands and at their mercy. "I ask you to note," I said, "that I am a prisoner of war, duly admitted to quarter."

"And why not?" the last speaker retorted with a curse. "Ain't we going to take you to Head-Quarters? And the shortest way?" with a wink at the others.

At this there came an interruption from the outer room. "Why don't you bring the d—d Tory out?" cried a voice that scorned disguise. "What's the use of all this palaver, Levi? Might be a Cherokee pow-wow by the sound of it. Come! If he don't know what to expect he'd best go and ask at Buford's! Bring him out, confound you! Here's his horse, and a rope and —"

"You'll let me dress?" I said. There was no chance, I saw, but clearly what chance there was lay in coolness and delay, if delay were possible. "With a long journey before me, a man likes to start handsomely," I continued, addressing the smaller man whom they called Levi. "I am sure that Captain Wilmer would not wish to put me to more inconvenience than is necessary. He's been at a good deal of trouble —"

"A vast lot too much," the man in the outer room struck in. "He needs a lesson, too, and we're the lads of mettle to give it him! Here," with a mingling of sarcasm and impatience, "pass along my lord's vally, and his curling tongs! 'Fraid we can't stop while he powders! Now, no nonsense, damme! Where's his clothes? Where's that nigger? Tom!"

The nigger was passed in from one to another, getting some rough usage on the way. "If you could withdraw, gentlemen, for a minute?" I said. Alone I might think of something.

But, "No, stranger, by your leave," Levi replied, with a sneer. "You're too precious! We're not going to lose sight of you till — till the time comes. Go on with your dressing, if you don't want to go in your shirt!"

Perhaps it was as well that they did not go, for I I was shaky on my legs and I feared nothing so much as that I should break down through bodily weakness. Their presence braced me and gave me the less time to think. Tom's fingers trembled so much that he was not as useful as he might have been, but with his help I got somehow into my clothes — with many a twinge and one groan that I could not check. The injured arm was already bound to my side, but by passing the other arm through the sleeve of a coat — Wilmer's I suppose, for my uniform was not wearable — and looping the garment loosely round my neck, I was clothed after a fashion. With these men looking sombrely on, and their shadows, cast by the wavering light of the candle, rising and falling on the ceiling, and the hurry and silence, broken now and again by some, "Lord ha' mercy" from the outer room, it was such a toilet as men make in Newgate but surely nowhere else.

"That'll do," Levi cried by and by. "You'll not catch cold."

"We'll answer for that!" chimed in another. "Bring him on! He'll be warm enough where he's going! We've wasted more time than enough already!"

My head swam for a moment. Then, thank God, the dizziness left me and I got myself in hand. I thought it right to make a last protest, however useless. "Note," I said, raising my head, "all here that I go unwillingly. These gentlemen do not intend me to reach Salisbury, and I warn them that they will be answerable to Captain Wilmer and to the Authorities for what they do. I am well known to Lord Cornwallis —"

"Enough of this palaver!" roared the brute in the outer room. "Are you turning soft, Levi? Why don't you bring the man through? If he won't catch cold, my mare will. Make an end, man!"

It was useless to say more. "Don't touch me," I said. "I can walk."

I went out in the midst of them into the living-room which I had not yet seen with my eyes. There, in the lamplight the fourth man was standing on guard over the negro women of whom there were three or four. Apart from them, with her back to us, and looking through a window into the darkness, stood Madam Constantia. I had not heard the girl's voice since the men had entered the house, and so far as I could judge she had carried out her threat, had uttered no protest, taken no side. She had deliberately stood aloof. Now, one does not look for protection to women. But that a woman, a girl should stand aside at such a time, should stand by, silent, unmoved, unprotesting, while her father's guest was dragged out to death — when even the negroes about her were moved to pity — seemed to me an abominable thing, a thing so unnatural that it nerved me more than I believe anything else could have. If I were English, and she hated me for that, she should at least not despise me! If she thought so ill of the King's officers that to her they were but milksops, she should at least find that we could meet the worst with dignity. She was abominable in her hardness and her beauty, but at least I would leave a thought to prick her, a something by which she should remember me. Better, far better to think of her in this pinch, than of home, of Osgodby, of my mother!

There would be time to think of these in the darkness outside.

As I entered the room — and no doubt, half-dressed as I was, I looked pale and ill — the women cried out. At that the men would have hustled me through the outer door without giving me an opportunity of speaking; but I managed to gain a moment. Mammy Jacks was blubbering — I called her to me. "My purse and what little money I have," I said, "is under my pillow. It's yours, my good woman. If Captain Wilmer will be good enough to let Lord Cornwallis know that Major Craven — Major Craven, can you remember — but he will know what to say. And one moment!" I hung back, as the men would have dragged me on. "There are some letters with the purse from a woman named Simms, who is about the Barracks at Charles Town. I want her to know that her husband is dead — was killed in my presence. I promised him that she should know. She should get a pass on the next Falmouth packet, and — you won't forget — Major Craven — my address in England is in the purse." Then, "I am ready," I said to the men.

I would not look again at the girl's still figure; I went out. Half-a-dozen horses stood in the darkness before the house, watched by a fifth man. One of these was thrust forward, and from the edge of the porch I was able, though weakly and with pain, to get into the saddle. The men mounted round me. They would have started at a trot, but I told them curtly that I could not sit the horse. On that they moved away, grumbling, at a walk.

I cast a backward glance at the long dark line of the house, and especially at the lighted window in which the girl's figure showed as in a frame. She was watching us go, watching to the last without concern or pity. Certainly she had warned me, certainly she had done her best to persuade me to go while there was time. But in the bitterness of the moment I could not remember this. I could only think of her as unfeeling, unwomanly, cruel. I had read of such women, I had never met one, I had never thought to meet one; and I would think of her no more. I knew that in leaving the house I left my last hope behind me, and that outside in the night, in the power of these men, I must face what was before me without a thought of help.

A man dismounted to lower a sliprail, and even while I told myself that there was no hope I wondered if, crippled and weak as I was, I might still find some way to elude them. Clopety-clop, the horses went on again. The night wind rustled across the fields, crickets chirped, the squeal of some animal in its death-throe startled the ear. Clopety-clop!

I tried to direct my thoughts to that future now so near, which all must sometime face. I tried to remove my mind from the present, so swiftly ebbing away, and to dwell on the dark leap into the unknown, into the illimitable, that lay before me. But I could not. Hurried pictures of my home, of my mother, of the way in which the news would reach Osgodby — these indeed flitted across my mind. But though I knew, though I told myself, that escape was hopeless, and that in a few minutes, in an hour, according as these ruffians pleased, I should cease to exist, hope still tormented me, still held me on its tenter-hooks, still swung my mind

61

hither and thither, as the chance of reprieve distracts the poor wretch in the condemned cell.

What if I broke away, one-armed as I was, and thrust my way through the men, taking my chance of obstacles? It would be useless, reason told me; and it might be the thing which they wished. It would absolve them from the last scruple, if any scruple remained. And at best I must be recaptured, for I knew neither my horse nor the country. Then — the mind at such times darts from subject to subject, unable to fix itself — I caught a word or two spoken by the riders in front.

"We can get one at the smithy," Levi said.

"Confound you, you make me mad," the other grumbled. "Why break our backs just to put him — " I missed the last word or two.

"You're a fool, man! We must give Wilmer no handle," Levi replied. "Let him suspect what he pleases, he can't prove it. If he can't show —" his voice dropped lower, I lost the rest.

So they were afraid of Wilmer, after all! But what was it that they were going to get at the smithy? And if we stayed there, was there any chance of help? I thought of Barter and the frightened women. Reason told me that there was no hope in them.

We were on the road now, riding in thick darkness under trees. The pain in my shoulder was growing with the motion, and from one moment to another, it was all I could do to restrain a groan. Frogs were croaking — cold for them I thought, with that strange leap of the mind from one subject to another. The men were silent, and save for the trampling of the horses and such sounds as I have named, the night was silent. How far were we going? Why need they be at the trouble of riding, and I at the pain, when the end, soon or late, would be the same?

Ha! there, before us was the faint glow of the smithy fire. Apparently the forge was at work to-night. It had not been lighted on the night of the King's Mountain fight.

As we sighted it, one of the men spoke. I caught the word "Spade." It was that which they were going to get at the smithy, then? A spade!

The word chilled my blood — I shivered. The glow of the smithy fire grew stronger as we advanced, the ring of a hammer on metal reached us. The men seemed to be disturbed by something and spoke low to one another. They even drew rein for a moment and conferred, but on second thoughts they moved on. "It can't be old Barter," said one. "But I'm mighty surprised if there was a fire when we came by. Who's lit it?"

"Perhaps his lad's come back?"

"Jake? Maybe. We'll soon know."

They drew up towards the forge at a walk.

When we were twenty yards from the doorway whence the light issued, a man strolled out of the shed, his hands in his pockets. He stood in the glow of the fire, looking towards us; doubtless he had heard the sound of the horses' hoofs above the clink of the hammer. He had a cigar in his mouth, and as he stood watching our approach he did not remove it, nor take his hands from his pockets. He stood quietly watching us, as we came towards him.

"Halloa!" said Levi, as we pulled up two or three paces from the stranger. "Lit the forge, have you?"

"Cast a shoe," the man replied. He was a small man, plainly, but, for the up-country, neatly dressed, and wearing a black leather jockey-cap. A rather elegant finical little man he seemed to me, and unarmed. Such as he was, my hopes flew to him, and rested on him, though in the way of help old Barter could scarcely have seemed less promising.

" You alone?" Levi asked, looking him over.

"You've said it," the man replied placidly. His eyes traveled from one to another of us. He did not move.

Levi bent his head and looked under the low eaves of the smithy. "You ride a good horse," he said. "A d—d good horse!" he repeated in a rising voice.

The man nodded.

Levi glanced over his shoulder. "Fetch it," he said to one of his followers — and I knew that he meant the spade, not the horse. Then, "What are you doing here?" he asked the stranger.

It was on this that the first real hope awoke in me. The man's calmness in face of this bunch of armed men — he had never removed his hands from his pockets or the cigar from his mouth — and a certain gleam in his eyes, that gave the lie to his mild manner — these two things impressed me. And his answer to Levi's question.

"I'm just looking round," he said gently.

For a moment I think that Levi was on the point of turning on his heel, and letting the man go his way. But his greed had been roused, I suppose, by a second look at the stranger's horse; and "That's no answer," he said roughly. ": What's your errand here? Who are you? What are you doing? Come!" he continued more violently. "We want no strangers here and no spies! We've caught one already, and it's as easy, s'help me, to find two halters as one!"

"And there are plenty of trees," the man answered coolly, with his eyes on me. "No lack of them either! Spy is he. He might well be English by the look of him."

"We'll take care of him!" Levi retorted roughly. "Who are you? That is the point! You're none of Shelby's men, nor Campbell's! Where do you live?"

"Well, I don't live here."

"Then —"

"Do you know Wilmer? Captain Wilmer?" the stranger asked.

"Yes, but — "

"He knows me. Ask him."

I struck in before Levi could make the angry rejoinder which was on his lips. "I am Captain Wilmer's prisoner," I cried, thrusting my horse forward. For the moment I forgot pain and weakness. "And I take you to witness, sir, whoever you are, that I am no spy, and that these men have carried me off from Captain Wilmer's house."

"D—n you, hold your tongue!" cried one of the other men, pushing forward and trying to silence me.

"I am Major Craven of the English Army!" I persisted. "I am a wounded man, taken at King's Mountain, and given quarter, and these men —"

One of them clapped his hand on my mouth. Another seized my horse's head and dragged it back. They closed round me. "Knock his head off!" cried Levi. "Choke him, some one!"

"That man, Barter — the smith!" I shouted desperately — the old man had just come to the smithy entrance — "he knows! He saw me with Captain Wilmer! Ask him!"

I could say no more. One of the men flung his arm round my neck and squeezed not only my throat but my shoulder. I screamed with pain.

"Take him on! Take him on!" Levi cried furiously. "I and Margetts will deal with this fellow. Take him on!"

"Stop!" said the little man; and more nimbly than I had ever seen it done, he whipped out a pistol, cocked it, and covered Levi, who was sitting in his saddle not three paces from him. "Don't take him," he went on. "And stand still. If a man goes to draw his weapon I shoot."

Never was a surprise more complete. The man who had tried to choke me let his arm fall from my shoulder, the men's mouths opened, Levi gaped. Not a hand was raised among them.

"Wilmer's prisoner, is he?" the little man went on; he spoke as quietly as he had spoken before. "And you were going to hang him? Mighty hurried, wasn't it?"

"What the h——ll is it to you?" Levi cried.

The muzzle rose from his breast to his head. "Better tell that man of yours to be still!" the stranger said — this time he spoke rather grimly. Then to me "Taken at King's Mountain, sir?"

"Yes," I said. "I've a broken arm and my shoulder was crushed. I appeal to you to rescue me from these men. If you leave me in their hands —"

The man stopped me by a nod. He took his cigar from the corner of his mouth, threw it away and substituted for it something that gleamed in the light. He whistled shrilly.

"Better stand still!" he said, as one or two of the horses backed and sidled, "I miss sometimes, but not at three paces." He whistled again, more loudly. "On second thoughts, you'll be wise to take yourselves off," he added.

"Not before I know who you are," Levi retorted with an oath. His mean face was livid with anger — and fear.

"Well, I'll tell you," the stranger answered in the tone of a man making a concession; and to my astonishment he dropped the muzzle of his pistol, cooly uncocked it, and returned it to his pocket. "I am Marion of Marion's Rangers, Marion of the Pee Dee River. My men will be here presently and if you take my advice you will be gone before they

68

come. There are plenty of trees about and we have ropes. I will be responsible for your prisoner," he added sternly. "Leave him to me."

Levi gasped. "Colonel Marion!" he cried.

"At your service, sir. Captain Wilmer is acting as my guide and if he finds you gentlemen here he may have something to say to this matter. Bring out my horse, my friend," he continued. addressing the old smith.

I rode clear of Levi's gang, no one raising a hand or attempting to stay me. I ranged myself beside Marion. Levi and his men conferred in low voices, their heads together, their eyes over their shoulders.

Marion turned his back on them while the smith brought out his horse, a beautiful black thoroughbred. I did not wonder that at the sight of it Levi's greed had been whetted. "I'd have shod him with gold," Barter said as he held the stirrup, "if I'd known whose he was, Colonel — and a little bit for his own sake. I might have known when I saw him, as he carried no common rider."

"Thank you, my friend," Marion said as he settled himself in the saddle. "I won't offer to pay you."

"God forbid!" cried the old man.

Marion turned to the five scowling, angry men who still held their ground. Even they were ashamed, I fancy, to back down before one man. "Gentlemen," he said in a small hard voice. "When I say, Go! I mean, Go."

"You're not on the Pee Dee now!" one of the men answered with insolence. ·

"You can tell that to my men." he replied. "When they come."

Far off, breaking the silence of the night, the beat of hoofs came dully to us. Levi heard it, and he turned his horse's head, and muttered something to his men. "Another day!" he cried aloud — but only to cover his retreat. Then he and these four brave men moved off with what dignity they might. The beat of hoofs came more loudly, and clearly from the eastward. The five began to trot.

Marion laughed softly. "They are grand folks — in a tavern!" he said.

A man who has had such an escape as I had had, and whose throat aches as he thinks of the rope that he has evaded, is not at his best as an observer. If he is capable of thought at all, he is prone to think only of himself. But I had heard so much of the partisan leader, whose craft and courage had defied the energy of Tarleton, and whose name was a terror to our people from the Pine Barrier to the ocean, and from the Santee River to the Gadkin, that I could not take my eyes off Marion. His marvellous escapes, the speed of his horse which was a fable through the Carolinas, the stern discipline he maintained, and his humanity to royalists and regulars alike — these things had already made his name famous. Pursued to his haunts in the marshes of the Pee Dee, he issued from them the moment the pressure was relaxed; and while Sumter and Davy and Pickens, all leaders of note, harassed us on our borders, it was Marion who sapped the foundations of our power, cut off our detachments, and harried our friends to the very gates of Charles Town. Tarleton, whom he had evaded a dozen times, called him the Swamp Fox, and grew dull at his name. But Tarleton could bear no rival, friend or foe, and carried into war a spirit far too bitter. For most of us Marion's exploits, troublesome as they were and rapidly growing dangerous, were a theme of generous interest and admiration.

He saw that I was observing him and probably he was not displeased. But after a moment's pause, "Are you in pain, sir?" he asked.

"Not more than I can bear," I replied. "Nor in any that should deter me from acknowledging the service you have rendered me."

"I am glad it fell out so," he replied courteously. "Here is Wilmer."

CHAPTER V

THE SWAMP FOX

Giving the rein to the most intrepid gallantry and in battle exhibiting all the fire and impetuosity of youth, there never was an enemy, who yielded to his valor, who had not cause to admire and eulogize his subsequent humanity. — It would have been as easy to turn the sun from his course as Marion from the path of honor.

GARDEN.

Wilmer rode up to us a minute later, followed by two horsemen, rough wild-looking men, who wore leather caps like their leader's. When he saw who Marion's companion was even his aplomb was not equal to the occasion. He stared at me open-mouthed. "What diversion is this, Major?" he cried at last. "You here? What in the name of cock-fighting are you doing here?"

"I am afraid Major Craven has considerable ground for complaint," Marion said, a note of sternness in his voice.

"Which Colonel Marion has removed at risk to himself," I said politely. "I am afraid that if it had not been for him I should have had no throat to complain with! A man called Levi and four

72

others entered your house an hour ago, Captain Wilmer, and dragged me out, and in spite of all my remonstrances —"

"Were going to hang him," Marion said grimly. "Fortunately they called at the forge, I was here, and Major Craven appealed to me. I interfered —"

"And they cried 'King's Cruse,' I warrant you!" Wilmer struck in.

"Well, they withdrew the stakes," Marion said with a ghost of a smile. "They were not a very gallant five. So all is well that ends well — as it has in this case, Wilmer. In this case! But —"

"But what was Con doing?" Wilmer cried turning to me. "That she let them take you out of the house?"

I fancied that the moment he had spoken he would have recalled his words; and acting on an impulse which I did not stay to examine, "She did what she could, I have no doubt," I answered. "What could she do? Colonel Marion may think little of facing five men —"

"Five corn-stalks!" he interpolated lightly.

"But for a woman it's another matter! A very different matter!"

"And yet," Wilmer said — but I thought that he breathed more freely — "Con is not exactly a boarding-school miss. She's —"

"She's my god-daughter for one thing," Marion said with a smile.

"I should have thought that she could manage a cur like Levi!"

"And four others?" I said. "Come, come!"

He shrugged his shoulders, but I saw that he was relieved by my words. "Well, it's over now," he said, "and she will tell us her own tale. I have no doubt that she did what she could. For the rest, I'll talk to Levi, Colonel, be sure. I am with you, that we have had too much of this. But that can wait. The Major looks shaken and the sooner he's in bed again the better. Never was a man more unlucky!"

"I am afraid that others have been still more unlucky," Marion said gravely. And I knew that he referred to some incident unknown to me. "But you are right, let us go. I am anxious to see my god-daughter and almost as anxious to see a pair of sheets for once."

He said good-night to the old smith and we started. Marion and Wilmer rode ahead, I followed, Marion's two men brought up the rear. So we retraced the way that I had traveled an hour before in stress of mind and blackness and despair. The night cloaked me in solitude, stilled the fever in my blood, laid its cool touch on my heated brow;

74

and far be it from me to deny that I hastened to render thanks where, above all, thanks were due. I had been long enough in this land of immense distances, of wide rivers and roadless forests — wherein our little army was sometimes lost, as a pitch-fork in a hay-stack — to appreciate the thousand risks that lay between us and home, and to know how little a man could command his own fate, or secure his own life.

Clop, clop, went the horses' hoofs. The same sound, yet how different to my ears! The croak of frogs, the swish of the wind through the wild mulberries, the murmur of the little rill we crossed — how changed was the note in all! Deep gratitude, a solemn peace set me apart, and hallowed my thoughts. How delicious seemed the darkness, how sweet the night scents — no magnolia on the coast was sweeter! — how fresh the passing air!

But as water finds its level, so, soon or late, a man's mind returns to its ordinary course. Before we reached the house, short as was the distance, other thoughts, and one in particular, took possession of me. What face would the girl put on what had happened? How would she act? How would she bear herself to them? And to me?

True, I had shielded her as far as lay in my power. I had given way to a passing impulse and had lied;

partly in order that her father might not learn the full callousness of her conduct, partly because I wished to see her punished, and I felt sure that no punishment would touch her pride so sharply as the knowledge that I had been silent and had not deigned to betray her. I wanted to see her punished, but even before revenge came curiosity. How would she bear herself, whether I spoke or were silent? Would she own the truth to her father? Would she own it to Marion of whom, I suspected, she stood in greater awe? And, if she did not, how would she carry it off? How would she look me in the face. whether I spoke. or were silent?

As we drew up to the house the lighted windows still shone on the night, and a troop of dogs, roused by our approach, came barking round us, after the southern fashion. But no one appeared, no one met us; doubtless the white men had ordered the negroes to keep to their quarters. Wilmer, who was the first to reach the ground, helped me to dismount. "But keep behind us a minute," he said. "We need not give my daughter a fright."

I assented gladly, hugging myself; I was to see a comedy! I stood back, and Marion and Wilmer mounted the porch and opened the door. Cries of alarm greeted them, but these quickly gave place to exclamations of joy, to cries of "Missie! Missie, he come! Marse Wilmer come!"

I pressed up to the doorway to see what was passing. Mammy Jacks was pounding at the door of an inner room — doubtless her mistress's. The other women with the vehemence of their race were kissing the Master's hand and even his clothes. "Steady! Steady!" Wilmer was saying, "Don't frighten her!" And he raised his voice,

" Con, it's I!" he cried. "All is well, girl. Here's a visitor to see you!"

She appeared. But I saw at a glance that this was not the same girl who on the night of my arrival had met Wilmer with flying skirts and cries of joy. This girl came out, pale, shrinking, frightened. True, in a breath she was in her father's arms, she was sobbing in abandonment on his shoulder. But, believe me, in that short interval my desire for vengeance had taken flight; it had vanished at the first sight of her face. The sooner she knew that I was safe, the better! I did not understand her, she was beyond my comprehension, she was still a puzzle. But I knew that she had suffered, and was suffering still.

"There, honey, all's well, all's well!" Wilmer said, soothing her. I think that for the time he had completely forgotten me and my affairs. "What is it?

What's amiss, child? Here's your god-father — a big man now! Look up, here's Marion!"

On that I crept away. I felt that I ought not to be looking on. It seemed to be a — well, I gave it no name, but I felt that I had no right to be there, and I went down into the darkness below the veranda, and stood a dozen yards away where I could not hear what passed, or could hear only the one sharp cry that the news of my safety drew from her. Marion's men had taken the horses round to the cabins, and I was alone. I had the puzzle to amuse me still, if I chose to work upon it; and I had leisure. But it was no longer to my taste and not many minutes passed before Wilmer summoned me.

I had no choice then, I had to go up into the room. But so changed were my feelings in regard to this girl that I loathed the necessity. I was as unwilling to face her, as unwilling to shame her, as if I had been the criminal. I would have given many guineas to be a hundred miles away.

I might have spared my scruples for she was not there, she was not to be seen. Instead, I met the men's eyes; they glanced at me, then away again. They looked disconcerted. For my part I affected to be dazzled by the light. "It has been a little too much for my daughter," Wilmer said. "I don't quite understand what happened," he continued awkwardly, "but she seems to think, Major — she seems to have got it into her head —"

"It was a shock to Miss Wilmer," I said. "And no wonder! I am not the steadier for it myself."

"Just so," he replied slowly. "Of course. But she's got an idea that she did not do all —"

"I hope that they did not strike her," I said.

It was a happy thought. It suggested a state of things, wholly different from that which was in their minds. Wilmer's face lightened. "What?" he said. "Do you mean that there was any appearance of — of that?"

"A cur like that!" I said contemptuously. "A devil of a fellow in a tavern!" I looked at Marion whose silence and steady gaze embarrassed me. "Or among women!"

"Ah!"

"But you must pardon me," I said. "I am done. I must lie down or I shall fall down. My shoulder is in Hades. For God's sake, Wilmer, let me go to bed," I continued peevishly — and indeed I was at the end of my strength. "You are worse than Levi and company!"

They were puzzled I think. They could not make my story tally with the words that had escaped her. But, thus adjured, they had no choice except to drop the subject, and attend to me. I was helped to bed, Tom was summoned, my shoulder was eased, I was fed. And they no doubt had other and more important things to consider than how to reconcile two accounts of a matter which was at an end and had lost its importance. I heard them talking far into the night. Their voices, subdued to the note of caution, were my lullaby, soothed me to slumber, went murmuring with me into the land of dreams. While they talked of ferries and night attacks, of Greene replacing Gage, of this man's defection or that man's persistence, of our weakness here and strength there, of what might be looked for from the northern province and what might be feared in Georgia, I was far away by the Coquet, listening to the music of its waters, soothed by the hum of moorland bees. The vast and troubled ocean that rolled between my home and me was forgotten. Alas, of the many thousands who crossed that ocean with me, how few were ever to return! How few were destined to see the old country again!

Late in the night I awoke and sat up, sweating and listening, my arm throbbing violently. And so it was with me until morning, fatigue imposing sleep, and jarred nerves again snatching me from it. At last I fell into a calmer state, and awoke to find the sun up and Marion standing beside me. His bearing was changed, he was again the leader, watchful, distant, a little punctilious.

"I make no apology for rousing you," he said. "I have to leave. I have discussed your position with Captain Wilmer and he will be guided by my advice. I could take you north to-day and see that you were conveyed safely to our Headquarters; but you are in no condition to travel. It would be barbarous to suggest it. I propose therefore to leave you here. In a month I or some of my people will be passing, and the opportunity may then serve. In the meantime I must ask you to give me your parole not to escape, while you remain here."

"Willingly," I said. "From the present moment, Colonel Marion, until — it is well to be exact?"

"Until I take you into my charge," he replied rather grimly. "Once in my hands, Major, I will give you leave to escape if you can."

"Agreed," I said laughing. "Have you the paper?"

He handed it to me. While he brought the ink to the bedside, I read the form and found it on all fours with what he had said. I signed it as well as I could with my left hand — the exertion was not a slight one. Then, "One moment," I said, my hand still on the paper, "How am I to be saved from a repetition of yesterday's outrage?"

"It will not be repeated," he answered, his face stern. "I have taken steps to secure that." I handed him the paper. "Very good," he continued. "That is settled then?"

"No," I said, "not until I have thanked you for an intervention which saved my life."

"The good fortune was mine," he replied courteously. And then with feeling, "Would to God," he cried, "that I could have saved all as I saved you! There have been dreadful things done, damnable things, sir, in the last week. The things that make war — which between you and me is clean — abominable! And they are as stupid as they are cruel, whether they are done by your people or by mine! They are the things of which we shall both be ashamed some day. For my part," he continued, "I believe that if the war had been waged on either side, with as much good sense as a Charles Town merchant, Horry or Pinkney, brings to his everyday business, the States would have been conquered or reconciled these twelve months past! Or on the other hand there would not have been one English soldier south of the St. Lawrence to-day!"

I smiled. "My commission only permits me to agree to the first of your alternatives," I said. "But I owe you a vast deal more than agreement. I won't say much about it, but if I can ever serve you, I hope, Colonel Marion, that you will command me."

"I accept the offer," he said frankly. "Some day perhaps I shall call upon you to make it good." And then, "You were with General Burgoyne's force, were you not?"

"I was," I answered. "I was on his staff, and surrendered with him at Saratoga. I have been — unlucky."

"Confoundedly unlucky!" he rejoined with feeling. "North and South!"

"Miss Wilmer," I began impulsively, "seemed to think —," and then I stopped. Why had I brought in her name? What folly had led me into mentioning her?

He saw that I paused and he shrugged his shoulders. He seemed to be willing to let it pass. Then he changed his mind, and spoke. "Do you know her story?" he asked. "She lost her mother very unhappily. Mrs. Wilmer was staying for her health at Norfolk in Virginia in '76, when your people bombarded it — an open town, my friend. The poor lady, shelterless and in such clothes as she could snatch up, died later of exposure. My god-daughter was devoted to her, as she is to her father. Women feel these things deeply. Can you wonder?"

"No," I said gravely. "I don't wonder. I knew nothing of this."

"I am sorry to say that that is not all," he went on. "Her only brother, a lad of eighteen, fell into your hands in the attack on Savannah. He was embarked, with other prisoners, for the West Indies. He has not been heard of since, and whether he is alive or dead, God knows. These things eat into the heart. Do you wonder?"

"No," I said, earnestly, "I don't! But in heaven's name why did they not tell me? I am known to the Commander in Chief, I have some small influence. I could at least make inquiries for them. Do they suppose that after the treatment I have received at Captain Wilmer's hands — though it be no more than the laws of war require — do they suppose that I would not do what I could?"

He looked at me a little quizzically, a little sorrowfully. "I am afraid," he said, "that all British officers — and all British sympathizers — are not like you. They have come here to deal with rebels." His face grew stern. "They forget that their grandsires were rebels a hundred years ago, their great grandsires thirty years before — and rebels on much the same grounds. They think that nothing becomes them but severity. Ah, we have had bitter experiences, Major Craven, and I do not deny it, some nobles ones! Your Lord Cornwallis means well, but he has much to learn, and he has made big mistakes."

I evaded that. "I will write at once," I said.

He raised his head sharply. "No!" he replied. "I am afraid, I must put an embargo on that. I have to think of Wilmer, and —" He checked himself. "He does not want a troop of horse to pay him a visit," he added, rather lamely.

"Of course, I should not say where I was," I answered, a little piqued. "Captain Wilmer may see the letter."

"Of necessity," Marion rejoined dryly. "But there are circumstances" — he hesitated — "this is a peculiar case, and I can run no risks. There must be no writing, Major Craven. I will see that news of your safety is sent in to Winnsboro'."

"Lord Cornwallis is at Charlotte."

"He was," Marion replied with a smile. "But your affair at King's Mountain has touched him in a tender place, and yesterday he was reported to be falling back on Winnsboro' as fast as he could. In any case, word shall be sent to his quarters wherever they are, that you are wounded, and in safe hands. That will meet your wishes?"

"I am afraid it must," I said grudgingly. "If you insist?"

"I do," he said. "It may seem harsh, but I have reasons. I have reasons. It is a peculiar case. And now, good-bye, sir. In a month I hope to travel north with you."

"Or rather I with you," I said, sighing.

"It's the fortune of war," he replied with a shrug, and that alert movement of the hands which sometimes betrayed his French origin. "Wilmer is going with me to-day, but he will return to-morrow or the next day. Then you will have company."

He took his leave then, and though he had treated me handsomely and I had reason to be grateful to him, I looked after him with envy. He was free, he was about to take the road, he had plans; the world was before him, already a reputation was his. And I lay here, useless, chained by the leg, a prisoner for the second time. I knew that I ought to be thankful; I had my life, where many had perished, and by and by, I should be grateful. But as I thought of him trailing over the flanks of the wind-swept hills, or filing through the depths of the pine-barrens, or cantering over the wide, scented savannahs, my soul pined to go with him; pined for freedom, for action, for the vast spaces with which two years had made me familiar. That I sighed for these

86

rather than for home or friends was a token perhaps of returning strength; or it may be that the sight of this man, who within a few months had written his name so deeply on events, had roused my ambition.

Be the cause what it might I found the day endless. It was in vain that Tom fretted me with attentions; I was useless, I was a log, any one might look down on me. To be taken twice! Could a man of spirit be taken twice? No, it was too much. It was bad enough to stand for that which was hateful, without also standing for that which was contemptible.

It was a grey rainy day such as we have in England in July after a spell of heat; soft and perfumed, grateful to those abroad but dull to the housebound. And Wilmer was gone. I heard no voices in the house, no spinning-wheel, the business of the plantation was no longer transacted within my hearing. There was nothing to distract me, less to amuse me. I fumed and fretted. When my eyes fell on the Bible which Madam Constantia had sent me, it failed to provoke a smile. Instead, the sight chilled me. How deep must be the enmity, how stern the purpose that could foresee the night's work, and foreseeing could still send that book!

I asked Tom if I could get up. He answered that I might get up on the morrow. Not to-day.

"But I am feeling much stronger," I said.

"Want no flust'ations," he replied. "Marse take dose sassaf'ac tea now."

I swore at him and his sassafras tea. "You v'ey big man ter-day," Mammy Jacks said.

"And pickaninny yesterday," I rejoined angrily.

This time she did not answer. Instead she grinned at me.

Presently, "Isn't Miss Wilmer well?" I asked.

"She sorter poorly," Mammy Jacks said. "She skeered by dat low white trash," with a side glance at me, to see how I took it.

"Isn't she afraid that they may return?" I asked.

"Marse Marion see to dat," the woman said, with pride. "He mighty big man. He say de wud, dey not come widin miles o' the Bluff! You des hev de luck uv de worl'," Mammy Jacks continued. "Dey hang nine, ten your folks day befo' yistiddy."

"Oh, confound you, you black raven!" I cried, "Leave me alone."

It was grim news; and for a time it upset me completely. For a while the service which Marion had done me and Wilmer's humanity were alike swept from my mind by a rush of anger. The resentment which such acts breed carried me away, as it had carried away better men before me. I cursed the rebels. I longed to strike a blow at them, I longed to crush them. I hated them. But what could I do, maimed and captive as I was? What could I do? Too soon the wave of anger passed and left behind it a depression, a despondency that the grey evening and the silent house deepened. I had escaped, I had been spared. But they, who might have been as helpless and as innocent as myself, and guilty only of owning the same allegiance, had suffered this! It was hard to think of the deed with patience, it was pain to think of it at all; and I was thankful when at last the night came, and I could turn my face to the wall and sleep.

But no man is fit to be a soldier who cannot snatch the pleasures of the passing moment; and when the next day saw me out of doors, when I found myself established on the veranda and the view broke upon me, liquid with early sunshine, and my gaze travelled from the green slopes that fringed the farther bank of the creek to the wooded hills and so to the purple distances of the Blue Ridge — the boundary in those days of civilization — I felt that life was still worth living and worth preserving. From the house, which stood long and low on a modest bluff, a pasture, shaded by scattered catalpas, dropped down to the water, which a cattle track crossed under my eyes. On the left, in the direction of the smithy, the plantation fields lay along the slope, broken by clumps of live oaks and here and there disfigured by stumps. On the right a snake-fence, draped with branches of the grape-vine, enclosed an attempt at a garden, which a magnolia that climbed one end of the veranda and a fig tree that was splayed against the other, did something to reinforce. All under my eyes was rough and plain; the place differed from the stately mansions on the Ashley River or the Cooper, as Wilmer himself differed from the scarlet-coated, periwigged beaux of Charles Town, or as our home-farm in England differed from Osgodby itself. But a simple comfort marked the homestead, the prospect was entrancing, and what was still new and crude in the externals of the house, the beauty of a semi-tropical vegetation was hastening to veil. At a glance one saw that the Bluff was one of those up-country settlements which men of more enterprise than means were at this time pushing over the hills towards the Tennessee and the Ohio.

That Wilmer was such a pioneer I had no doubt, though I judged that he had more behind him than a dead level of poverty. Indeed I found evidence of this on the little table that had been set for me beside my cane chair. It bore a jug of spring water, some limes, and a book in two volumes. I fell on the book eagerly. It was *The Rambler*, published in London in 1767. Now for a house on the distant Catawba to possess a copy of *The Rambler* imported some education and even some refinement.

No one but the girl could have put the book there; and had she done this before the news of the murder of my comrades reached me I should have received the act in a different spirit. I should have asked myself with interest in what mood she proffered the boon, and how she intended it; whether as an overture towards peace, or a mere civility, rendered perforce when it could no longer be withheld.

But now I was too sore to find pleasure in such questions. What softer thoughts I had entertained of her, thoughts that her agitation and her remorse on the evening of the outrage had engendered in me, were gone for the time. I found her treatment of me, viewed by the light of other events, too cruel; I found it too much on a par with the acts of those who had murdered my comrades in cold blood. I forgot the story of her mother and her brother. I believed even that I did not wish to see her.

For I had not yet seen her. As I passed through the living-room I had caught a glimpse of Miss Lyddy's back; who, unprepared for my visit, had fled and slammed a door upon me, as if I were indeed the French. The negro women had grinned and curtsied and cried, "Lord's sake!" and fussed about me, and been scolded by Mammy Jacks.

But of the girl I had seen nothing as I passed through.

Doubtless she was on the plantation taking her father's place and managing for him. And doubtless, too, I must presently see her. For at the farther end of the veranda, where the glossy leaves of the magnolia draped the pillars and deepened the shade, was a second encampment, a chair, a table, a work-basket; and beside these a spinning-wheel and an old hound. Nor even if she shunned this spot, could she long avoid me. Though I sat remote from the doorway, no one could enter or leave the house without passing under my eyes.

I fancied that after what had passed she would not be able to meet me without embarrassment, and for this reason, she might choose to surprise me; she might come out of the house and appear at my elbow. But two hours passed, the beauties of Johnson were losing their charm, even the prospect was beginning to pall on me, and still she did not come. Then at last I saw her on the farther side of the creek, coming down to the ford — a slender figure in white, wearing a broad hat of palmetto leaves. A black boy carrying a basket ran at her side and two or three dogs scampered about her. She was armed with a switch, and she crossed the stream by a line of stepping-stones that flanked the ford.

I watched her with a mixture of curiosity and indignation, as she tripped from stone to stone. She had to mount the slope under my eyes, and I had time to wonder what she would do. Would she come to me and speak? Or would she pass me with a bow and enter the house? Or would she ignore me altogether?

She did none of these things. I think that she had made up her mind to bow to me as she passed. For at one point, where she was nearer to me, she wavered ever so little, as if she were going to turn to me. Then a flood of red dyed her face, and blushing painfully, sensible I am sure of my gaze, but with her head high, she crossed the veranda and entered the house.

"Well, at least she can feel!" I thought. And if I regretted anything, it was not that I had stared at her, but that she might not now choose to come to me. She would not soon forgive the humiliation of her.hot cheeks.

CHAPTER VI

ON PAROLE

"But who can tell what cause had that fair maid
To use him so that loved her so well"?

SPENCER.

A moment later the girl proved that her sensibility was less or her courage higher than my estimate, for just as I had pictured a little earlier, she surprised me. I found her at my elbow, and I rose to my feet. Unluckily as I did so, I struck my injured arm against the chair, and she — winced.

That might have disarmed me, but it did not. I remembered the nine men who had been murdered in cold blood, and I thought of my narrow escape; after all I was not a dog to be hung without ceremony and buried in a ditch! And now she was in my power, now, if ever, was the time to bring home to her what she had done. Still, she was a woman, I owed her courtesy, and I endeavored to speak with politeness. "I see that you are more merciful," I said, bowing, "in fact than in intention, Miss Wilmer."

Her agitation was such — she did not try to hide

it — that for a moment she could not speak. Then "If you knew all," she said in a low voice, "you would know that I had grounds for what I did, Sir."

"That you had good grounds, I cannot believe," I answered. "And for knowing all, I think I do. I know that you have suffered. I know that you have lost your mother and your brother. I know that you have grievances, sad grievances it may be against us."

"You don't know all," she repeated more firmly.

"But I know enough," I rejoined — I was not to be moved from my purpose now. "I know that I was your father's prisoner and your guest; and that you stood aside, you did not raise a hand, not a finger to save me, Miss Wilmer. You did not speak, though a word might have availed, and I believe would have availed to preserve me! You let me go out to a cruel death, you turned your back on me —"

"Oh, don't! don't!" she cried.

"You quail at the picture," I retorted. "I do not wonder that you do. I was your guest, I was wounded, I was in pain, alone. Has a man, when he is maimed and laid aside, no claim on a woman? No claim on her forbearance, on her pity, on her protection? For shame, Miss Wilmer!" I continued warmly, carried farther than I intended by my feelings. "Men, when their blood is hot, will plan things, and do things, God knows, that are abominable. But for a woman to consent to such, and, when it is too late, to think that by a few tears she can make up for them —"

"Stop!" she cried — I suppose that I had gone too far, for she faced me now, hardily enough. "You understand nothing, sir! Nothing! So little that you will scarcely believe me when I say that if the thing were to do again—I would do it.";

"I cannot believe you," I said coldly.

"It is true."

I stared at her; and she returned my look with a strange mixture of shame and defiance. "Why?" I said at last. "In heaven's name, why, Miss Wilmer? What have I done to you? Your mother I know. But had I a hand in it? God forbid! Was I within a hundred miles of it? No. Your brother — and there again, I find that hard to forgive. Your father had spared my life, sheltered me, brought me here; could you not believe that I was grateful? Could you not believe that I would do much to serve him and something to repay him? That all that it was in my power to do for your brother, by my exertions or my influence, I would do? But you did not tell me. You did not ask me?"

"No," she said.

"Why?" I asked bluntly. She did not answer. "Why?" I repeated. I was at the end of my anger. I had said what was in my mind and said it with all the severity I could wish. And I was sure that I had made her suffer. Now I wanted to understand. I sought for light upon her. There was a puzzle here and I had not the clue.

But she stood mute. Pale, forbidding, not avoiding my eyes but rather challenging them, and very handsome in her sullenness, she confronted me. At last, as I still waited, and still kept silence, she spoke. "And after I had told you?" she said. "If you had offered help, would it then have been easier to — to stand aside?"

"And let me go to my death?"

"Yes," she said.

"Good God!" I cried. I could not check the words, I was so deeply shocked. If she had deliberately considered that, she was indeed determined, she was indeed ruthless; and there was nothing more to be done. "I am sorry," I said. "I had thought, Miss Wilmer, that I might say what was in my mind and then let the thing be as if it had never been. I wished to speak and then — to let there be peace between us. I thought that we might still come to be friends. But if we are so far apart as that, there can be nothing between us, not even forgiveness."

"No," she answered—but her head sank a little and I fancied that she spoke sadly. "There can be nothing between us. Nothing, sir. We are worlds apart."

Before I could reply Mammy Jacks came to summon her. One of the blacks wanted her, and she broke off and went into the house.

She left me adrift on a full tide of wonder. What a woman, I thought! Nay, what a girl, for she was not more than twenty, if she were not still in her teens! If all the women on the Colonial side were like her, I thought, if but a tithe of her spirit and will were in them, the chances of poor old England in the strife which she had provoked were small indeed! I could compare the girl only to the tragic heroines of the Bible, to Judith, or to Jael, who set her hand to the nail and her right hand to the hammer. Very, very nearly had she driven the nail into my temple!

And yet she had, she must have a gentler side. She had broken down on that night, when she thought that the deed was done. I could not be mistaken in that; I had seen her fling herself in a passion of remorse on her father's breast. And then how strong, how deep was the affection which she felt for that father! With what tenderness, with what tears and smiles and caresses had she flown to his arms on his return from the field!

98

She was a provoking, a puzzling, a perplexing creature; and alas, she began to fill far more of my thoughts than was her due. I was idle, and I could not thrust her from them. Because she did not come near me I dwelt on her the more. The chair at the other end of the veranda remained empty all that day and the next, and it was not until noon of the third day that I again had a word with her. Then, as she passed by me with her head high, she saw that something was lacking on the little table on which I took my meals, and she fetched it herself. I wished to bring on a discussion; and as she set the thing down, " Thank you," I said politely. "But can I be sure that I am safe in eating this?"

She did not fire up as I expected. "You think that I may poison you?" she said, making no attempt to evade the point.

"Well, you told me," I replied, somewhat taken back, "that you were prepared to do it again, you know?"

She sighed. "If I meant it then, I do not mean it now," she said. "I have done all that I can. I leave the rest to God!"

Certainly she said the most singular things! However, what surprise I felt I hid, and I tried to meet her on her new ground. "That being so," I said smoothly, "why should we not bury what is past — for the time? I have to live for a month under your roof, Miss Wilmer. We must see one another, we must meet hourly and daily whether we will or not. Cannot you forget for a month that I am an enemy?"

"No," she answered with the utmost directness, "You are an enemy. Why should I pretend that you are not? We are rebels and we are proud of the name. You are of those who are paid to reduce us, to make war on us" — her color rose, her eyes dilated as she spoke — "to burn our towns, to waste our fields, to render our old homeless and our children motherless! And why? Because you are false to your traditions, false to your liberties, false to that freedom for which your forefathers died, and for which we are dying to-day!"

The spirit, the tone, the brooding fire in her eyes filled me with admiration. But I was wise enough to let no trace of this escape me. "I cannot admit that," I said, "naturally."

"No," she replied swiftly. "Because you are paid to see it otherwise."

"At any rate you are frank, Miss Wilmer," I said. "And you really do see in me the mercenary of a cruel tyrant?" I smiled as I said it, and I flattered myself that the jest pierced her armor. At any rate she lost countenance a little. "And I suppose I ought to see in you a rebel," I continued. "But it may be that I do not in my heart think much worse of you for being a rebel. And it is possible that you do not think so very badly of me for being — paid!"

"It does not sound well," she said with disdain.

"No," I replied. "Beside romance, duty sounds poorly, and makes a dull show."

"The tea-duty does!" she exclaimed viciously — and saw before the words were well said that her wit had betrayed her into familiarity. She colored with annoyance

I seized the chance. "And what of it?" I said. "Tolls and taxes and the like! What are they to us here? If I admit that a tax, which has turned thirteen loyal colonies into what we see, was an unwise one, surely, if I admit that, you may admit that it is hard for a proud nation to retrace its steps."

"I am not concerned to admit anything," she answered haughtily.

"Still if that is all that is between us?"

"It is not!" she exclaimed. "It is not!" For a moment she stood a prey to strong agitation. Then she muttered again, "It is not all!" and she went deliberately away from me. But she went like one under a heavy burden or the weight of a distressing thought.

MADAM CONSTANTIA

Still I was not ill-pleased with the result of our interview. She had stepped down from her pedestal. She had left for a while the tragic plane on which she had hitherto moved and from which she had stooped to me. I had climbed a step nearer to her. In future she would not find it so easy to keep me at the distance that suited her pleasure and that, at the same time whetted my curiosity.

And perhaps something more than my curiosity. For I could not deny that, handsome and perplexing, cold, yet capable of ardor, she had taken a strong grip upon my thoughts. I could not keep her out of my mind for an hour together. A dozen times a day I caught myself looking for her, listening for the sound of her voice, watching for her appearance. The morning was long, the hour dragged that brought neither the one nor the other. Nay, there were times — I was idle, be it remembered, and crippled — when the desire to bridge the distance between us and to set myself right with her became a passion; when I would have given very much for a smile from the averted face, or a look from the eyes that passed coldly by me.

It was absurd, but I have said I was idle. And yet after all was it so absurd? I compared her with the women whom I had known at home; with the women of fashion with their red and white cheeks, their

102

preposterous headdresses, their insipid talk of routs and the card table; or again with our country-bred hoydens, honest and noisy, with scarce an idea beyond the stillroom or the annual race meeting: and I found that she rivaled the former in dignity and the latter in simplicity. Adorable, inexorable creature, she was well named Constantia! I was glad — such a hold was she getting on my mind — when her father returned, two days later than he had said, and brought news that distracted my thoughts.

The check at King's Mountain had stopped Lord Cornwallis in his advance on North Carolina. He had fallen back and established himself again at Winnsboro', so that he was still not more than sixty or seventy miles from us. "If your bone were set, I should send you north, Major," Wilmer said with a look more than commonly thoughtful. "But I fancy that your friend, Tarleton, has learned his lesson from Ferguson, and won't stray far from Headquarters. And now Greene has taken over Gates's command — "

"Is that so?"

"It is — he won't leave your people so much time to look about them. I do not think that they will journey as far as this, but if I thought they would, you would have to travel, my friend, fare as you might."

103

That with a little more, not to the purpose, was the only talk I had with him for some days. And presently I conceived the idea that this was no accident. I began to suspect that Madam Constantia, not content with sending me to Coventry herself, was bent on keeping him from me. I came even to think that I owed to this desire on her part the fact that I now saw something, though little more, of her. For she would interpose between us rather than let me talk to him. If her father, as he crossed the veranda or came in from the fields had the air of drifting towards me, she was sure to see it, and to draw him aside, sometimes by a word, more often by a look, rarely by speaking to me herself. More than once when he approached me — he was in his cynical way a good-natured man — she appeared so pat to the occasion that I gave her the credit of watching us, and believed that her eyes were upon me more often than I knew.

I fancied even that there was an understanding between them on this point. For when she surprised him in my neighborhood, though he might have stood only to say "Good morning!" or "Good fall weather!" he would wear an air half guilty and half humorous, as of a child caught transgressing. And once when this happened, I had a queer illusion. It seemed to me that the look of amusement that

Wilmer shot at the girl, and which I was not meant to catch, transformed his face in the most curious way. It shortened it, vulgarized it, widened it. For a moment I saw him no longer as the shrewd, lean Southerner he was, but as a jovial, easy, smiling person, for all the world like an English yeoman or innkeeper. The fancy lasted for an instant only, and I set it down to the shadow cast by his hat or to a tricky cast of the sunshine as it shimmered through the leaves of the magnolia behind him. But later I thought of it more than once. The change in the man, though passing, was so great that I should not have known him for himself; and it haunted me.

I believe that it was about three days after this, when he was abroad upon the plantation, on which he spent most of his time, that Madam Constantia and I came again to blows. Time lay heavy on my hands — he may be thankful who has never known the aimless hours and long tedium of the prisoner — and though I had no prospect of forwarding letters, I thought that I would amuse myself by learning to write with my left hand. It was not a thing to be done in a moment, but Mammy Jacks provided the means and I fell to the task in the leisurely way of an invalid, now scrawling a few words in round hand, now looking away to the purple distances that reminded me of our Cheviots on a fine October day, and now lazily watching the blacks who were trooping past, bringing in the last of the cotton. It was sunny, it was warm, and the slaves in their scanty white clothes with baskets on their heads formed a picture new to me. I was gazing at it, pen in hand, when the girl came through the veranda, glanced my way, and in a twinkling descended on me like a whirlwind.

She snatched away the paper that lay under my hand and before, taken by surprise, I knew what she was about, she tore it across and across.

"Ungrateful!" she cried. "Have you forgotten your parole, sir? Were Colonel Marion here, you would not dare to do this!"

"To do what?" I retorted, rising to my feet. I was as angry as she was. "What should I not dare to do?"

"What you are doing!" she rejoined, her eyes sparkling and her breast heaving with excitement.

"I am learning to write with my left hand. Why not?"

"Why not?" she exclaimed. "And what did you promise Colonel Marion?" She pointed to the paper which she had flung on the ground. "What did you undertake on your honor?"

"That I would not communicate with my friends," I answered sternly. "Nothing more!"

"And what are you writing?" she cried. But her tone sank by a note, and uncertainty fluttered in her eyes.

"That is my business!" I answered. "What is it to you, pray, what I write? Or see!" I stooped, and with difficulty owing to my stiff arm, I recovered one of the scraps of paper. "See! Satisfy yourself. It is but a tag from the book that you lent me."

She took it. "'Sure such a various creature ne'er was seen!'" she read mechanically, and with a falling face. "'Sure — '" she stopped.

"Is it sufficiently harmless?" I asked ironically. "Is there dishonor in it? At least I can say this — I know of no one here, Miss Wilmer, to whom the words can be applied. From your father I have met with consistent kindness and attention. And from you equally consistent — but I will not define it. I leave you to judge of that."

She was now as angry, I believe, with herself as with me; but she did not see how she could retract and for that reason, whatever the original cause of her attack, she would not own herself in the wrong. "I believe there is such a thing," she said stubbornly, "as cipher writing."

I stared at her with all the contempt I could throw into my gaze. "Cipher writing!" I said. "Certainly I have come into this wilderness to learn strange things! Cipher writing! But enough — and too much!" I continued wrathfully. "I am not used to have my honor doubted. When your father returns I shall refer the matter to him and I shall ask him if I am to be assailed under his roof— assailed in a manner as insulting as it is outrageous!"

"I will ask him myself," she said in a much lower tone. "If I am wrong I am sorry. But Colonel Marion told me —"

"That I was not to communicate with my friends? Am I doing it? But, no," I concluded loftily, "I will not discuss it. I will refer the matter to your father."

And I turned my back on her without much courtesy — the attack was so wanton, so silly! I heard her move away and go into the house.

She was crazy, positively crazy, I thought. What was it to her whether I wrote or did not write? What was it to her if I did communicate with my friends? She was not my keeper, she could not judge of the risk or the importance of the step which Marion had forbidden. Placed as we were within less than seventy miles of the British Headquarters and within the scope of a cavalry raid, he was doubtless right in making the stipulation. But what did she know of it? What was it to her? Why should she attach importance to the matter?

Confound her impudence! I might be one of the bare-footed slaves trudging through the heat, I might be a wretched Sambo fresh from Guinea, and she could scarcely treat me with greater contumely. She was a fury, a perfect fury, and as passionate as she was beautiful! But I would speak plainly to Wilmer. I would tell him that I was his prisoner, and owed something to him, but that I could not, and would not, be subject to his daughter's whims and caprices. Write? Why should I not write? Sheets, quires, reams if I pleased, so long as I did not forward. And how in heaven's name was I to forward? Through whom? Did she suppose that the postman called once a day as in Eastcheap and Change Alley? The whole thing was monstrous! Monstrous!

I waited, fuming, for Wilmer's return from the fields, and meantime the delay brought to my mind another grievance, though one which I could not name. I had supposed that when he came back, after leaving Marion, I should be invited to make one at the common table. But no invitation had reached me, my meals were still served apart, and this seemed absurd in a house in which life was pleasantly primitive. Certainly this was a minor complaint. But he who has lived for months with men whom a common danger has rendered respectable but could not render congenial, he to whom a woman's voice has grown strange and the decencies of home a memory, will understand what I felt when scraps of Aunt Lyddy's chatter, the girl's grave voice, the cackle of Mammy Jack's laughter came to me — outside.

A small grievance and one that I could not air, one that I must keep to myself. But it rose vividly before me. I was sure that it was not Wilmer, I was sure that it was the girl who shut me out and would have none of my company.

Noon came without bringing Wilmer, and soon I guessed that Madam had played a trick on me. She intended to keep us apart. At that the anger which time and thought were cooling, flamed up afresh, and I longed to thwart her.

Hitherto I had limited my exercise to a turn or two in front of the house. But I saw no reason why I should not go farther, and seek Wilmer in the fields where the blacks were picking. After dinner, accordingly, I chose my time and set out. She should not have it all her own way. If he would not come to me I would go to him.

I had to cross the horse-paddock and the rails were up. They were heavy, I had only one arm, and bandaged as I was I could neither stoop freely, nor use my strength such as it was; for now I moved

I found to my disgust that I was only half a man. I tried to shift the upper rail, but a pang that brought the sweat to my brow shot down my arm, and I desisted. The sun beat down upon me, the flies swarmed about my head, the din of the crickets filled my ears. I leant upon the rail, enraged at my helplessness but unable for the moment to do more.

I was in that position when she found me.

"You must come in," she said. "Let me help you." I suppose I looked ill for there was a tone in her voice that I had not heard before.

"I wish to go on," I said pettishly, turning from her that she might not see my face. "I am going to your father."

"You must come in," she replied firmly. "The sun is too hot for you. You have never been as far as this."

"But I —"

"You must do as I say," she insisted. "Lean on me, if you please. Don't you know that if you fell you might hurt yourself seriously?"

"I am only a little — giddy," I said, clinging to the rail. "Which — I don't seem to see — the way?"

I went back to the house on her arm — there was nothing else for it — but the only incident of the journey that I could recall was that at a certain place I stumbled, and she held me up. I tried to laugh. "A — a milksop! A weakling!" I said.

She did not answer.

When she reached the house she put me into my chair on the veranda, and disappeared. She returned with a glass of Madeira. "You must drink this," she said, "you are not used to the sun"; and she stood over me until I had done so. Then when the giddiness had passed off and things were clear, "My father tells me," she continued hurriedly, "that I must ask your pardon. He says that I ought to have taken it for granted that you would keep your word — that nine out of ten English officers — "

"Would do so?" I said stiffly. "We are much obliged to him."

"And that men can tell very quickly when they can trust one another."

"As a rule they can."

"I will bring you some more paper," she said meekly. "And I beg your pardon."

"Please don't say any more," I replied. "Can you not believe, Miss Wilmer, that I am grateful — most grateful for what has been done for me? And that, enemy as I am, I would not willingly injure the meanest person in this house."

"I do believe that," she said in a low voice.

112

"You do?" I cried, pleased at the concession. "Then surely — "

"But you might have no choice in the matter," she replied gravely. "Honor — " she paused, looking away from me, apparently in search of a word — "is a two-edged weapon. It protects us to-day, sir. It may wound us to-morrow."

"If you mean," I answered, "that after I am exchanged I shall fight against you, it is true. But we can fight without ill-will and suffer without rancor. While we observe the rules of the game, we are brothers-in-arms though we are in opposite camps. That is the legacy, Miss Wilmer, that chivalry has left to us."

She seemed to think this over. "And honor?" she resumed, her face averted. "It binds always, I suppose? It imposes rules which it is not possible to evade, no matter what the exigency may be? If you had to choose between your mother's life — shall I say? — and your honor, what then, Major Craven?"

"I cannot conceive the situation," I answered, smiling at the absurdity of the idea.

"You might be on parole as you are to-day," she rejoined. "Suppose that your mother's life depended, no matter how, on your presence, on your breach of your word? What would you do? Would you still put your honor first?"

"I do not know what I should do," I answered.
"The thing is apart from ordinary experience. But
I know what my mother would say. She would
say, 'Keep your word!'"

She was silent for a moment. "And to betray
your country even in a small matter, that too
would be a breach of honor, I suppose?"

"I am afraid that it would be a very bad one,"
I answered, smiling. "If you are thinking of bribing
me to disclose our secrets, I had better tell you at
once that I have no secrets, Miss Wilmer."

"And if you had you would not sell them?"

"Neither sell them, nor tell them. I hope not."

"No," she replied. "I do not think you would."
I heard her sigh deeply. Then, "I will take your
glass," she said. And she took it and went into
the house.

She left me puzzled, puzzled to the last degree;
but at the same time I felt that the girl had come
nearer to me. She left a picture of herself a little
different from that which I had hitherto possessed.
Perhaps it was the hat, the wide-brimmed shadowy
hat that softened her features and by taking from
her height, lowered the stately carriage of her head.
Perhaps it was the vague elusive sadness of her tone.
Perhaps something else. She had named my
mother. I wondered what my mother would think

of her, with her perplexing ways, her reserve, her aloofness, the hostility which she had not stooped to veil. Often my mother had said in jest that she did not know where I should find a wife, since I looked shyly on our country belles, and she would have none of our town ladies. To which my father had answered that such fastidiousness generally ended in a milkmaid — and that he believed that the next Lady Craven would be no better.

A milkmaid? Would they consider — I lost myself in wild and extravagant dreams. Blowsabella? Surely no one could be less like a Blowsabella. Or for the matter of that less like· the Hartopps our neighbors, who talked of nothing but plaited bits, lived in riding coats, and romped through a country dance like so many Dulcineas del Toboso!

No, no one could say that she was a milkmaid. On the other hand I doubted if she had ever seen a Panache — the latest headdress — or held cards at Loo, or squalled a bar of Sacchini's music, or chattered down players and pit at a tragedy. She belonged to no category. She was herself, and an odd, troubling, haunting self at that!

CHAPTER VII

HICKORY KNOB

For I must go where lazy peace
Will hide her drowsy head,
And for the sport of Kings increase
The number of the dead.

But first I'll chide thy cruel theft
Can I in war delight?
Who being of my heart bereft
Can have no heart to fight?

DAVENANT.

I don't know how long I had been lost in these musings when Wilmer's return to the house put an end to them. As he crossed the veranda, carrying his gun and followed by a black boy trailing two wild turkeys after him, he turned as if he were going to join me. But he changed his mind at the last moment and paused some paces from me. "It's a pity it's that arm, Major," he said. "There's a glut of turkeys in the woods. But you've had other sport at home, I hear?"

A little offended I put a question with my eyes.

He grinned. "They're hard to understand are women," he said. "Beyond you and me, Major. We'll say no more than that."

116

He nodded and went on, entering the house before I could answer. But again I had that queer passing impression of another man, a jovial, easy, talkative fellow, fond of a glass and a toast. Perhaps it was his smile. A smile would naturally shorten a man's face. Perhaps it was the sunlight. Or perhaps it was just a fancy that had taken hold of me. Wilmer, like most Southerners, had humor of a kind, but he was certainly neither jovial nor talkative, and I should not have described him as an easy companion. His wit was of the dry and caustic sort, that leaves the person addressed at a disadvantage.

He left home again three days later — to join Davy's band I gathered; and I had seen so little of him, while he was at the Bluff, that I did not miss him. I was beginning to recover my strength and from day to day I went farther afield. Sometimes I passed the ford and wandered up the pasture, a vast park-like meadow, broken by clumps of oaks and chestnuts, trees that in that country mark good soil as poplars indicate a poor site. Or I might venture into the forest and amid the undergrowth of sweet-scented myrtle and dog-wood and honey-suckle — and other shrubs less healthy — I would put up a deer or come on the tracks of a bear; or in the sombre twilight of the pine woods, with their melancholy festoons of gray moss, I would hear the tapping of the Southern woodpecker. Aunt Lyddy made friends with me and talked of Braddock and Washington and Wolfe and the heroes of the last war; and at times would betray by a look of distress and a tremor of the hands that she was conscious that something was amiss in her world and that things did not consort with reality as they should. On these occasions the girl, if she were present, would humor her and reassure her with incredible tact and kindness; and at the same time she would dare me with stormy eyes to come within so much as a mile of explanation. Her patience with Aunt Lyddy was indeed the measure of her impatience with me. And set me far from her.

Yet at a distance we were better friends now. She never joined me where I sat on the veranda, but she would sometimes of an afternoon take her seat at the spinning-wheel at the farther end by the old blood hound; and I would, though timidly, wander that way and draw her into unwilling talk; at any rate it seemed to be unwilling on her side and it was certainly jejune. She never asked me to be seated, and seldom, while I was there, looked up from her task; but she would answer, and bit by bit I learned something of her family story. On her mother's side she was of French blood; it was on that side that she was akin to Marion, and the result was that she spoke French in a way that put me to shame. When she named her mother,

"You were greatly attached to her?" I ventured.

"She was my mother," she answered.

"And your father?"

"He is more to me than anything in the world," she replied with the same simplicity. "He was my mother's last charge to me."

"And no doubt you are often anxious about him?"

"Anxious?" For once she looked at me. And then in a tone of feeling, too tragic, as it seemed to me, for the occasion, "God knows how anxious!" she said. "God knows what is the weight I have to bear!"

I thought her answer over-strained. I thought her anxiety more than the occasion required; and I felt about for an explanation. "You are so near the fighting," I said lamely, for I felt that I was making excuse for her. "Doubtless it is more trying to you."

"I am so near," she answered with the same depth of feeling. "And so helpless! So helpless! I sit and wait! And wait!"

"That is too often the woman's part, I fear."

"God forbid," she replied with extraordinary

bitterness, "that my part should fall to the lot of many women. He cannot be so cruel!"

I drew away after that. I did not dare to press her farther, for I thought that she was overwrought and hardly herself. The note of tragedy seemed to be out of place in face of this calm country-side, of the still woods, of the lowing cattle, of the smiling negroes going about their tasks under our eyes.

But all our talks were not of this nature, and stoutly as she guarded the approaches to intimacy, there were times when I caught her in a gentler mood or by sheer meekness broke down the barrier of her reserve; so that perforce she grew more kind. At such times she listened while I talked of my home and my people and the England, which she knew only through the pages of Addison and Goldsmith and Richardson; or I described the long voyage with its stale water and sour beef which had brought me hither; or she spoke herself, not willingly, of the old plantation on the Ashapoo, of society on the French Santee, where she had visited the Marions, of her boarding school at Charles Town, of the Cecilia Society with its concerts, and the old Provincial Library. It was clear that Wilmer had been in better circumstances, but when I ventured to sympathize with her on her isolation her only answer was, "Give us peace! Only give us peace!"

"Peace?" I echoed. "Yes."

And I knew that I was losing my own peace. I knew that the pose of her small head, as it bent over the wheel or the needle, the slender grace of her figure, the proud sadness of her eyes were coming between me and the rest of the world; and that beside a kind look from those eyes, that now dwelt absently on things unseen by me, and now viewed me with a cold attention, hardly anything in life had any value for me, or any sweetness. Had I met her elsewhere and in ordinary conditions, I believe that I should have succumbed to her charm. But here, where she was the one woman, set in this lonely place as in a frame, encircled by the peace of green glades and scented hemlocks, by myrtle and reddening sumach, and where, besides, she walked a perplexing puzzle, a sphinx, a figure for vain imaginings — was any other issue possible?

A rebel? The daughter of a planter? I thought no more of such things. Here, where every morning I looked across the valley to the far-off mountains, where the endless spaces of the air smiled beneath my eyes, here, within touch of the primitive forest and the wide prairies, such distinctions lost their meaning. The busy life of the camp, the Norfolk Discipline — how often had I cursed it! — the jovial dinner, the ride, the foray, faded into a dream;

and even the quarrel which had brought us — a mere handful of pigmies, over the boundless ocean to this land, seemed no longer of moment, but a mere trifle, the play of children quarreling in some squalid alley of a distant town.

And whether in this, love opened my eyes or closed them, whether I now saw things by the light of truth or duped myself for a season, what matter? In a month from my coming I had waded in over shoes, over boots. For me the die was cast and I knew that I dreaded nothing so much as the day that should see my back turned on the Bluff. The old life had lost its savour and seemed, as I looked back, an impossible procession of dull routine and distasteful days.

Doubtless had I been French I must have spoken. But there is in us a vast force of silence. Where the Frenchman is proud we, until a certain day comes, are ashamed of passion. And apart from the distance which she maintained between us, there was a dignity about Constantia as she moved in the midst of her household, and governed her slaves, that set all thought of love at defiance. I could not bring myself to believe that she regarded me as anything but an unlucky encumbrance, one of the evils of war. Indeed, as my arm improved and my strength returned, and I stood in less need of help or pity, I fancied that her intolerance of my presence grew and increased. She noted when the month that Marion had named came to an end. She showed trouble at his non-appearance, and fretted without disguise at the delay. At times she was ice to me. And then I, who would have given the world for a kind word from her lips, could have cursed her for her unconsciousness!

Not that I had not once or twice intoxicating moments. Once I looked up from my book as I sat on the porch and I found her eyes brooding upon me. For a few seconds mine held them — it seemed as if she could not drag hers away! Then, as she at last turned her head, I saw the blood dye the whiteness of her neck and cheek to the very hair; and for a delicious minute my heart rioted madly. Again I was standing over her one day and I had fallen silent, gazing at and worshipping her slender neck and high-braided head. I suppose she felt my eyes upon her, for slowly I saw the same blush spread over the white — slowly and irresistibly; and to stay the foolish words that rose to my lips I had to go away and hide myself in my room, where I sat gripping the cold fingers of my bandaged arm until the blood burned in them. Why, why had she blushed, I asked myself? For when I met her next, she was cold as Diana and distant as a star. And as if she were not satisfied with that, but must punish me farther, she presently sent to me to ask if I would be good enough to leave the veranda free next day, as she wished to examine a small parcel of a new staple of cotton. As the veranda was the only place where I had the chance of seeing her, this was enough to vex me; but I had no choice except to obey, and I spent the greater part of the morrow in my own room and in a bad temper. I was there about three in the afternoon fretting and fuming and trying to read when I heard the patter of naked feet crossing the porch, a sound that was quickly followed by a stir in the house. A moment later the commotion grew to something like an alarm. Voices rose here and there in various keys, I caught cries of affright, a door was slammed hurriedly, silence followed. And on that, to tell the truth, my heart sank.

"Marion is here," I thought. "He has come for me." And if Marion's return had meant release and freedom instead of a prison hospital at Hillsboro' I do not know that I should have been much better pleased!

I did not go out or make inquiry. I considered that I had been cast on my own company with little thought and small ceremony; and pride bade me wait until I was summoned. I clung, too, to hope as long as it was possible to do so. It might not be Marion. The stir might have nothing to do with me. And so some minutes, five perhaps, passed. Then with no warning there came a sharp knock at my door, and Mammy Jacks entered. The woman looked flustered and alarmed.

"Marse Craven," she said, "Missie, she up'n sond fer you. She des tarryin' fer you de no'th aidge uv Hick'ry Knob, en I 'low de sooner'n you go de better. A little mo' en you miss er en de kindlin'll be in de fier. You gwine?"

I stared at the woman. I fancied at first that I had not understood her. "Hickory Knob?" I said. "Why it is two miles from here! Madam Constantia cannot have walked there! I heard her voice less than —"

"Go 'long! Aint I done tell you she ridin' Injun Belle?" Mammy Jacks replied scornfully. "She tuck'n sond piccaninny fer you. You gwine ter go? Co'se," — she turned away with great dignity — "ef you hev udder fish ter fry, it's notin ter Mammy Jacks. She done tell you."

"Stop!" I said, my mind a jumble of impossible conjectures, "Don't be in such a hurry. I'll go, of course, if I can be of use. But I don't understand—"

"Dat's needer yer nor dar," Mammy Jacks

answered. "Ef you 'er too bigitty ter go, Marse, dar's an eend. Eh? You gwine? Clar to goodness den, sooner'n you skip de better! Ef you not fine Missie no'th aidge uv de Knob you ter wait an hour twel she come. Bimeby she trompin' round. She sholy boun' ter come."

I followed the woman from the room, still marvelling, still questioning, my head in a whirl. She hurried me through the living-room to the door at the rear of the house which looked towards the negroes' cabins — low huts of shingle, vine-clad, mushroom-like, dwarfed by the giant shade-trees that rose above them. Beside the house-door stood a black boy with a single cloth about him, who still panted from the speed at which he had come. His face was strange to me, and I asked if he were coming with me.

"Look like you know de track widout him!" the woman rejoined. "Aint you bin ter de Knob de las' week uz ever wuz? You better run 'long er Missie'll be dar befo' you! Den you'll hear mo' en you pleez'd ter like. Dat's w'at I'm thinking, Marse Craven."

I strode off without waiting for more, passed beside the cabins and skirted the negroes' patches of corn and vegetables. Beyond these I plunged into the woods, following a fairly-marked track. The

Knob was a rocky point, rising well over a hundred feet above the forest roof, some two miles southwest of the Bluff. I had visited it for the sake of the view which I was told its summit afforded; and I should have gone a second time if about the same distance northwest of the Knob, there had not risen above the trees another hill — King's Mountain. Its slopes were greener, it was more pleasant to the eye. But I knew that on those slopes, above which vultures and crows hovered in the air, the bodies of my fellows lay unburied. And that thought had been too much for me. I had not gone again.

But to-day that and all kindred thoughts were far from my mind as I pushed my way along the narrow track, now thrusting aside the scented plants that form in Carolina so large a part of the undergrowth, and now traversing the gloom of a pinewood where the feet sank without a sound in the rotting leaves. Even the heat and flies, even the scurry of a doe and fawn across my path were little heeded. My mind was in a tumult of wonder and conjecture. I thought only of Constantia, of her summons, of her possible need. I strove to imagine what had happened, what had, or could have, happened, to lead her to send for me; above all, I wondered what she could want with me at Hickory Knob, a place distant and solitary — she who had

127

never offered me her company abroad, never gone farther with me than to that sliprail?

Wondering, I sought the answer to these questions and sought it fruitlessly. I could find no answer that consorted with her character or was at one with her treatment of me. Had she met with an accident? She would not send for me. Had she fallen into hostile hands? I could do nothing, maimed and unarmed as I was. Was Marion with her? Then, why did he not come to the house? No conjecture that presented itself agreed with the facts, and I could only hasten my pace as much as my arm permitted, and look forward to seeing her.

Where should I find her? At the foot of the rock? Or at the summit? Or would she perhaps be waiting for me at a certain flat stone on a level with the tree-tops, which formed a convenient seat, and which a carpet of nutshells and broken corncobs pointed out as a favorite resort of the negroes? I could not tell. The tangle of forest vines about me was not more blind or more confused than were my thoughts.

I came at last, sweating at every pore, and fighting the swarms of flies that accompanied me to the foot of the little hill. She was not there; I could hear nothing. The stillness of afternoon lay heavy on the woods. Impatient of delay, I paused for a moment only, then I started to scale the hill and in less than a minute I stood beside the flat stone I have mentioned. She was not there, and I did not tarry, I climbed on, now slipping on the shale, and now clutching at branches of the myriad azaleas that earlier in the year clothed the bare hill with flame. At length I reached the summit which was no bigger than the floor of a barn.

She was not there and I stood awhile, glad to take breath and to cool my heated face. I looked abroad over the silent trees, over the carpet of forest which autumn was beginning to dye to its pattern. I viewed for a moment the smooth green head of King's Mountain, that to the westward rose above the trees. Then I turned to mark, in the direction whence I came, the cleft in the woods which marked the clearing about the Bluff. Beyond it the forest sank and was replaced by the more distant view of the mountains.

I waited, expecting, with each moment that passed, to hear the movements of her mare on the path. How would she look? What countenance would she put on? What would she, what could she have to say to me? I lost myself in a fever of anticipation. Ten minutes passed, twenty minutes, at last the full half hour! And still she did not come. Still there was no sign of her, no sound of her approach.

At length the heat of expectancy began to give place to the chill of doubt. Had I mistaken, could I have mistaken the place? Or was there another path up the Knob and could she be waiting for me at the foot of the farther side. I hurried across the top, I descended some distance, I called, I whistled. I strove to pierce the thickets with my eyes. Then, harassed by the thought that while I lingered, she might be mounting by the proper track, I toiled again to the summit and looked abroad. She had not appeared, and my heart sank. Doubt in its turn began to give place to suspicion. Had I been tricked? And if so, to what end? Desperately I searched the trees with my eyes. She might still come, but the hour I had been told to wait was nearly up. Indeed in no long time the sun would set, and twilight in Carolina is brief. If I remained on the Knob until it was dark, I should have small chance of returning through the woods without a fall that in my crippled condition might be serious.

I was now angry as well as suspicious. I had been duped — for some reason; duped by a trick too transparent to deceive a child. I had been sent out of the way; I had not a doubt of it now. I only wondered that I had been so easily gulled. Still I would not act in a hurry. They should not say that I had left the rendez-vous before the time. They should not have that excuse. So I waited fuming and fretting until the hour expired, and then reckoning that I should have no more daylight than would suffice for my return, I scrambled down the rocky slope, and in a state of cold anger very different from the heat of anticipation in which I had come, I made the best of my way towards home.

A man, and a soldier, does not like to be tricked. He does not choose to be treated as a child even for his own good. And in this case the lure which they had used, the bait which I had swallowed so greedily, seemed to imply a knowledge of my feelings that made me hot only to think of it. Had the girl been amusing herself with me? Had she, cold and distant as she seemed, been laughing at me? Worst of all, had she taken that d — d grinning black woman into her confidence? No wonder that as I labored on I cursed the boggy piece that delayed me, the roots over which I stumbled, the . thorns that snatched at my clothes?

I did not consider what I should say. My one longing was to confront them. But I had not reckoned with the darkness that fell earlier in the woods than in the open, and soon I had to pick my way for fear of a fall which might injure my arm.

When I came in sight of the cabins it was dusk and a light already shone from one of the windows of the house.

I was making for this light, with angry words on my lips, when a figure rose suddenly in the path before me and barred my way. It was Mammy Jacks. Apparently she had been crouching on the ground on the look-out for my coming.

"Fer de Lord's sake, stop, honey!" she jibbered, bringing her ugly face close to mine, her eyeballs and her teeth shining in the gloom. "Der's Cap'en Levi dar, en de udder rapscallions! Ef you go in, you no mo' chance den a rooster in de pan! Der ain't no Marse Marion ter 'elp you loose de rope dis time! Ain't you no eyes ter see de hosses?" And she clutched me by the arm and held me.

I did see then — with a decided shock — a row of saddled horses standing beside the porch, thirty yards from us. With them were a couple of men lounging, as if on guard. The row extended round the corner of the house so that I could not count either men or horses and the dusk made all indistinct. The windows, now that I was nearer, showed more than one light, though these were darkened from time to time as a figure passed across them. A murmur of voices, a stir of feet, the clink of glass, and now and again a loud laugh issued from the windows and mingled with the jingle of bit and stirrup-iron.

"See dat? W'at I tell you?" Mammy Jacks repeated in terror that was certainly not feigned; and she clung firmly to my sleeve. "You go in, en you sholy hang! Cap'en Levi, he mighty mad atter you en he make an eend dis time! Look like dey sarched de cabins, en you kin hide in dar! Hide in dar, Marse Craven! Fust thing you know de Cap'en'll get up en go. He go fer sho' in ten minutes."

I let her push me towards the door of the nearest hut; to hide there, as she said, seemed to be the wisest course for the present. But either the reek of the shack repelled me, or her insistence touched the wrong note. My pride rose and on the very threshold I turned. Why should I hide? I had Marion's word and the girl's word. And weeks had elapsed and nothing had happened since Levi's last attempt. Was this some new trick for my good for if so, I would not stoop to it. The part I had played at the Bluff had been poor so far; I was not going to make it worse and disgrace myself by hiding in a nigger's hut from a parcel of low rebels whom a single man with a pistol had put to flight.

"No!" I cried; and I resisted the woman's thrust.

133

"I'll be hanged if I do, Mammy! I'll see Levi and all his crew with their father the devil first!"

"Den you'll hatter hang!" she gibbered, struggling to detain me. "Fer de Lord's sake, honey, 'tend ter me! Don't go in dar!" she protested, her voice rising to a shriek. "Don't go in dar! Dey'll hang you fer sho! Dey'll — Marse Craven — fer de Lord's sake —"

But I wrested myself from her hands, I flung out of the hut. As I did so, some one in the house laughed aloud, a pair of hands clapped applause, a glass shivered on the floor. I was being tricked, I was sure of it now; and I bounded across the short space to the door, Mammy Jacks' wail of despair in my ears. I evaded a second figure that slipped out of the gloom and tried to stop me, I thrust open the door that was already ajar, and a pace inside the room I stood, confounded.

The table was spread for a meal and spread as I had never seen it laid at the Bluff, with glass and silverware and all that was rarest in the house. On it were meat and drink and whisky and even wine. At the head of the table staring at me with laughter frozen on her lips — aye, and with terror in her eyes — sat Constantia. At the foot was Aunt Lyddy, I believe, but I did not take her in at a first glance. For between them, seated at the table were three men

in regimentals that glittered with gold lace. Two
of them wore the green of Tarleton's British Legion,
one was in the King's scarlet. And my amazement
may be imagined when I saw that the one in scarlet,
was young Paton, my own particular friend on the
Staff! While of the others the nearer to me was
Haybittle, a grim, hard-bitten veteran, who had
never risen beyond a pair of colors in the regular
service, but now ranked in the Legion as a Captain.
I knew him well.

On both sides there was a moment of silence and
astonishment. I glared at them.

The first to recover from his surprise and to find
his voice was Paton. He pushed back his chair,
and sprang to his feet. "Who-hoop!" he shouted.
"Who-hoop! Run to earth, by Gad! Look at him,
Haybittle! You'd think he saw a ghost instead
of the King's uniform. Here's his health!" He
swung his glass round his head. "A bumper! A
bumper!"

I stood stock still. "But how — how do you
come here?" I stammered at last. I stared at Paton
in his scarlet, at the glittering table, at the candles
that shed a soft light upon it, but it was only the
girl's stricken face that I apprehended with my
mind. And even while I put the question to Paton,
my brain asked another — what did her look of

135

horror, of despair mean? "How do you come here?" I repeated. "You are not prisoners?"

"Prisoners!" Haybittle answered in his harsher tones. "Good G — d, no! We've come for you, Major, and a deuce of a ride we've had to fetch you! We'd pretty well given you up too!"

"Thanks to this young lady who lied to us!" the third man struck in. I knew him slightly — a New York Tory holding a commission in Tarleton's horse and like many loyalists more bitter than the regulars. "It would serve Madam right," he continued rudely, "if we burned the roof over her head! And for my part I'm for doing it!"

"Hold your tongue, Carroll!" Paton cried angrily. "You're always for burning some poor devil's house or playing some silly trick of that sort! Don't be afraid, Miss Wilmer," he continued, "You played your hand, and had a right to play it, and played it well! And by jove, such a face as yours, if you will allow me to say so, knows no laws. But I can tell you," he went on, addressing me, "my lady came pretty near to bamboozling us, Major! We were just toasting her in a last glass when you came in looking like Banquo's ghost — and damme, almost as pale! Five minutes more and we should have been off and away!"

"And we ought to be away now!" Haybittle said,

136

rising to his feet. "Sergeant! Get 'em to horse. Don't lose a minute!"

"I'm on parole," I said.

"Parole be hanged!" Haybittle answered bluntly. "We retake you! Hit in the arm, eh, Major? Well, you can ride and we've a horse for you. And ride we must as if the devil were behind us. I'm not for doing anything to this young lady," with an awkward look at her, "because she fibbed to us! But I don't trust her for that reason, and — "

"Steady, Captain Haybittle," I said, regaining my voice and my faculties — the girl continued to sit and look before her with the same stricken face. "This lady's father saved my life when I was wounded and helpless. He has sheltered me and treated me more than well, and more than humanely. Not a dog must be injured here, or a truss taken, or you will have to reckon with me. I am the senior officer here — "

"No, by G — d, you're not, Major," Haybittle retorted bluntly. "Not till your name's replaced on the active list, and that can't be till you have reported yourself at Headquarters as returned to duty. General Tarleton put me in charge of the expedition, and I'll give up the lead to no one — with all respect to you."

"And I'm for doing something! I'm for teaching

these rebels a lesson!" Carroll protested, encouraged by Haybittle's action.

"You'll learn a lesson yourself, Lieutenant," Haybittle rejoined, "and that pretty quickly if you don't see the men to horse. While we're mounting, throw forward vedettes as far as the smithy we passed. Off, man, and see to it!" Then to me, "We're thirty miles from Fishing Creek, where our supports are, and seventy miles from our lines. Green is at Charlotte, a deal too near us for my taste, and has thrown forward Sumter's men. I'll give you three minutes, Major, by my watch to get your things together — not a second more. We're only twenty, all told, and before we are ten miles from here we shall have the country swarming on our backs."

He hurried out. Carroll had already gone. Paton with a sly look at me and a glance at the girl — who still sat silent in her chair — went after him.

I approached her diffidently, "Miss Wilmer," I said, "have you nothing to say to me before I go?"

She awoke as from a dream. She met my eyes. "You are going then?" she said.

"I have no choice."

"And your parole — is nothing?"

"It is put an end to by my re-capture," I said. "Colonel Marion will understand that. But I want you to understand something more; that nothing — nothing can put an end to the gratitude which I owe to your father and to you. When it shall be safe for me to return —"

"To the Bluff?"

"Yes — for I shall return, Miss Wilmer, be sure of that. And when I do return to the Bluff I shall be free to tell you, and to prove to you —"

"How great is your gratitude!" she cried, rising to her feet and substituting other words for mine — for indeed it was of something more than gratitude I was going to speak. "Your gratitude?" she repeated, with a look and in a voice that cut me to the heart. "Will it be worth more than your word? Will it sever one of the meshes that bind you? Will it evade one of your cruel laws? Will it save one life? No, Major Craven! If the day comes for me to ask a return, to crave a favor, to plead to you, aye, even on my knees, I know that the law that frees you to-day will bind you then! And I shall find your gratitude no better than your word! For me, you can take it, sir — where it may mean more!"

She pointed scornfully to the old lady who sat, wondering and bemused, at the farther end of the table. And yet I doubt if Aunt Lyddy was more bemused at that moment than I was. The girl's outbreak was to me beyond all understanding. I was astonished, indignant, nay, sorely hurt! For what had I done. What beyond that which I was doing, could I do? "You are cruel, and unjust!" I cried. "What have I done that you should wound me, at this moment? Believe me, if you could read my heart, Miss Wilmer —"

"I do not wish to read it!" she answered passionately. "Take it there with your gratitude! I value both at their true worth!" Again she pointed to poor Aunt Lyddy who gazed at us, understanding nothing of the debate. And that was the end, for before, hurt and angry, I could find words with which to answer the girl or to reproach her, the opportunity was past. Haybittle bustled in, his sword clanking on the floor.

"Time! Time!" he cried. "You must come, Major. Not another moment!" He took me by the sound arm and forced me towards the door. "You are playing with lives," he continued, "and I don't choose to hazard mine for the sake of a girl's eyes. No offence to you, Miss," he flung over his shoulder. "You'd make a fine tragedy queen, be hanged if you wouldn't. To look at you one would think that we'd done God knows what to you, and a good many would! There's temptation and to spare. Now boot and saddle, Major! We've risked more than enough to get hold of you! Let us be going!"

CHAPTER VIII

THE MAN WITH TWO FACES

This outward sainted Deputy,
Whose settled visage and deliberate word
Nips youth i' the head and follies doth emmew
As falcon doth the fowl — is yet a Devil!

SHAKESPEARE.

Haybittle dragged me out. From the porch I had a last view of the room. It showed me the table set for a feast, as I had left it, the old lady seated in her chair, Constantia on her feet, motionless, and gazing after us. Was it fancy or did I read something besides scorn and defiance in the girl's eyes as they followed me; a shadow of fear, of appeal, of unutterable sorrow? I could not tell, and I had no time to dwell on the fancy. In a twinkling I was half-lifted and half pushed into the saddle of a troop-horse, the reins were thrust into my hand, the word was given, we moved off, the lighted windows faded as by magic. I had one glimpse of Mammy Jacks' face amid a knot of staring negroes, a moment in which to press my purse — once before given and returned — into her hand, and we had left all behind, and were filing down the field road, amid

141

the jingle of bits, the trampling of hoofs, the curt orders, all the familiar sounds of a troop of horse on the march.

I was among my own people, Paton's cheery tones cried, "Hark Forrard!" in my ears, his kind hand had knotted my spare rein to his saddle. I was free, with friendly hands and voices round me, and a good horse between my knees. I should have been jubilant, I should have been happy, I should have been content at least; and Heaven knows I was wretched. It was not only that we were parted, but in the moment of parting the girl had judged me unfairly and hurt me wantonly, God only knew why! She had flung my thanks in my face and poured scorn on the affection of which — for she was a woman — she must at least have had some suspicion.

Sore with the pain of parting, I cried out passionately against her injustice: that injustice which, had I been indifferent to her, must still have been cruel. As it was I loved her; and at this our last interview, when I had been on the point of telling her, hurried and ill-timed as the moment was, something of what I felt, she had — oh, but it was cruel! For I might never — I might never see her again. This might be my last memory of her.

Yet at this moment her stricken face, her eyes,

wells of grief and appeal, rose up before me, and gave me a strange bewildering certainty that I was loved. That I was loved! She might pour contempt on me, she might insult me; but the very violence of her language proved that there was something in her heart akin to that which swelled in mine. There was a bond between us. Miles might part us, but her eyes followed me, and her heart. For, here was the old mystery, the old puzzle. But of pain is born knowledge; and with her reproaches in my ears, and every pace of my horse carrying me farther from her — and never perhaps should I see her again! — I was sure at last that I had touched her heart.

Yes, out of my wretchedness I came suddenly to that knowledge. The eyes that had followed me had given the lie to the eyes that accused me. There was a mystery still, but — at this point Paton broke in upon my thoughts.

"Major, rouse yourself!" he cried in my ear. "Come, you've cheated the Jews and bilked the sponging house, and you're as mum as one of these confounded trimmers who are neither on one side nor the other! Cheer up! Your heart will be whole as soon as your arm,

Though now they are moaning on ilka green loaning
The flowers of the Forest are all wede away!

There I'll say no more! But you've never asked

143

how we came to find you? It was due to me, my lad, due to me! One of Ferguson's men came in a week ago. He'd been hiding by day and walking by night. He heard from some loyalists — few enough in this part! — who sheltered him, that there was a wounded officer lying at a plantation not far from King's Mountain. Greene had let us know you were alive — quite a courteous message it was — and putting two and two together with the help of a man who knew the district we fixed upon the place where we found you. But we did not say a word — far too much has crept out lately. I saw Tarleton and he consented to push ten miles up Fishing Creek, and to lie there thirty hours. He gave me Carroll and twenty men, but — in your ear, Major — Carroll's too much given to burning and harrying for my taste, and I insisted on having Haybittle as well, who's a good fellow, though not thorough-bred. And here we are!"

"How's my lord?" I asked, forcing myself — it was no small effort — to take an interest in things.

"He has gone down the country for his health for ten days; he has left my other lord in charge."

"Rawdon?"

"The same — and gallant old Webster to nurse him. Poor Ferguson's death has set us back damnably. You left us at Charlotte — Gates was then at Hillsborough a long way north. Now we're back at Winnsboro' and Greene, in Gates's place, and worth six of him, the devil take him! is at Charlotte. Sumter is out on the Broad, west of us, and Davy is across the Catawba east of us, and it was no small feat, Major, to slip in between them; they're no fools at the business. And we're not out of the trap yet. However, if you can ride through the night in spite of your bad arm, we shall be with Tarleton by daybreak. He's lying, as I said, on Fishing Creek where he defeated Sumter a couple of months ago, but he has a party out watching the fords of the Catawba and Davy will be clever if he surprises him.

"Where's Marion?" I asked. My curiosity was natural.

"Who can say?" Paton answered, shrugging his shoulders. "Wemyss has been hunting him on Lynch's Creek but to no purpose. Tarleton fancies that he's back on the Pee Dee now and far to the right of us. I hope it is so. He's a wily old fox, if you please."

"Well, I must do my best," I said, "but why have you let Davy and Sumter push in so close to us. That's not Tarleton's ordinary fashion."

"Because they've more friends than we have," Haybittle answered dryly. He had reined his horse back to us. "They don't know when they're beaten, these Southerners. Since we broke them up at Camden, hanged if things are not worse instead of better! Every hand is against us and some of the hands are in our dish., If we bring you off safe — which way is that fool of a guide turning?" He broke off to shout, "Look out, Carroll, where you are going! — it will be because we have kept a still tongue — a still tongue, Major, and told no one except Tarleton what we were doing!"

"Haybittle's right," Paton said. "Every movement we've made during the last month has been known to Sumter and Davy before we made it!"

"Aye, there's a leak in the vessel somewhere," Haybittle growled. "And it's one that nothing but a halter will stop — six feet of hemp is what is needed. My lord is altogether too easy. He is hail-fellow-well-met with too many of these loyalists. There is one or other of them at his ear from morning till night, and not a plan is made but, in place of keeping it to himself, he must needs discover the he of the land from some Jack Tory or other. My lord learns a little and the Tory learns more, and it is my opinion, he does not keep his knowledge to himself. It's either that, or we have a Benedict Arnold on our side. And then, the sooner we catch their André and hang him up the better. Sergeant!" raising his voice, "pass on to Lieutenant Carroll to be careful that he takes the right fork at the next ford, and loses no time in crossing that strip of hill! The moon is shining on it."

Trot, trot, trot, trot, through the mud, and up the slope! There is something in a night march across a hostile country, something in the caution which is necessary, in the low curt orders, and the excitement, which appeals strongly to the spirit of a soldier. In spite of the sudden halts and jolting starts which many a time put my fortitude to the test, in spite of sad thoughts — for surely to be misread by one we love is sharper than a serpent's tooth! — I began to take pleasure in what was passing. Whether we wound quickly over the flank of a hill with moonlight gleaming on spur and bit, or tracked the course of a stream through a fern-clad ravine, where the mimosas and the yellow jessamine scented the spray, or plunged knee-deep through a quaking bog where the clamor of the frogs covered the splashing of the horses, I owned the charm. Regret began to give place to ambition. Since I was free I longed also to be hale and strong. I yearned to be in the field once more. After all, life held war as well as love; war that on such a night puts on its fairest face, its garb of Border story; love that on such a march seems sad and

147

distant, bright and pure, as the star that gleams through the wrack of clouds above us.

The sun was an hour high when, a long line of crawling horses and weary men, we surmounted the last ridge and sighted far to the south of us the dark head of Rocky Mountain. Fishing Creek, the bridge, and the distant valley of the Catawba lay below us, and by and by we espied Tarleton's pickets thrown far out as was his custom. I could endure the shaking no longer, and at this point I slid from the saddle, and trudged down the last mile on my feet. From the Camp below rose presently a sound of cheering voices! The men had counted our number as we descended the face of the hill, and they had made us one more than had started on the expedition the day before. Ten minutes later the old flag waved over our heads, I was safe as well as free. Tarleton, with the courteous insouciance which was natural to him and which could at need give place to an unsparing energy, came forward to welcome me to his camp.

"My lord Rawdon's compliments, sir, and he will be glad if you will report yourself at his quarters."

"Very good," I said. "Does his lordship wish to see me at once?"

"I believe so, sir."

THE MAN WITH TWO FACES

"Very good, Tomkins. I will be with his lord-ship as soon as I can borrow a sword."

The order reached me early on the morning after my arrival at Winnsboro'. But owing either to the fatigue of the ride — though I had rested six hours at Fishing Creek — or to other causes, I had already begun to experience, early as the hour was, the lassitude and ennui which await the man, who after startling adventures returns to a dull routine. The scarlet of the King's uniform, peeping here and there through the trees that shaded the village street, the smart sentries who paced the walk before this door or that, the Twenty-Third drilling in an open space with their queues and ribbons and powdered heads, the old flag flying above Headquarters — these were sights pleasant enough. And the greet-ings of old friends were welcome; the camaraderie of an army campaigning abroad is a thing by itself. But when that was said, all was said. A camp is a camp, and the older it is the worse it grows. After the life of the Bluff, with its primitive cleanliness, its great spaces, its comfort and its stillness, the close air and squalor of billets, the shifts and dirty floors, the sharp orders and sounds of punishment, even the oaths and coarse talk to which custom had once in-ured me, jarred on me unspeakably. Nor was the distaste with which I looked about me, as I passed

149

along the village street, lessened by the thought that for some time to come my wound would withhold me from action and confine me to the narrow bounds of the camp.

I had not many minutes to spare for these or for any reflections. It was but a short distance, the length of a measured stroll, from the lodging where Paton had taken me in, to where my Lord had his headquarters, nearly at the end of the village. I soon arrived at the place, a low white house, set back a little from the street and separated from it by a row of fine shade trees which sheltered a rough table and some benches. There was the usual throng about the door, but I pushed my way through it, and the orderly who had summoned me, and who was on the look-out, ushered me without delay into my Lord's presence.

A man of my own age, twenty-seven or twenty-eight, was seated at the head of a table strewn with papers and maps. Webster, who commanded the Twenty-Third, sat at the foot of the table and between the two were ranged five or six men of varying ages, of whom one or two were not in uniform. I saw as much as this at a glance, as I crossed the threshold. Then my Lord rose and came forward to meet me with a cordiality that sat well on his years without derogating from his rank.

"My dear Craven," he said, shaking me by the hand, "welcome back to life! Tarleton has done some good work, but he has never done His Majesty's cause a greater service than by restoring you to it. Your arm? How is it?"

"Doing well, my lord," I murmured. And I thanked him.

"Excellent! Well, an express went to your father three weeks ago enclosed in the Commander-in-Chief's despatches, which told him of your safety. You will dine with me to-night and tell me about poor Ferguson's affair. Poor fellow! Poor fellow! But there, sit down now! No, gentlemen, you must keep your congratulations until later. Time presses and the matter we are on brooks no delay. Brigadier," he continued, addressing Webster, "find room for Major Craven beside you — and have a care of his arm. He is here just in time to be of service to us, and now —" He broke off, his attention diverted by a movement at the table. "What is it?" he asked, turning sharply in his chair, and extending his arm so as to bar the way to the door.

One of the men in civilian dress, who had risen from his seat at my entrance, muttered something. He would be glad of his lordship's permission to — and with a murmur and a low bow, he was for leaving the room.

But my lord stopped him. "No, sir," he cried peremptorily. "Sit down!" And without deigning to hear the man's reasons, he motioned him back to his chair. "Sit down, sir! Sit down! Nonsense, man we shall not be fifteen minutes, and your matter can wait. We may need you, we shall almost certainly need you. Now Major Craven, I require your attention. Am I right in saying that about three months ago you rode across the country that lies between the forks of the Congaree — from the Enoree to the Broad River? That is so, is it not?"

"I did, my lord," I said. "I spent three days in the district, mainly on the Tiger River."

"About the level of Fishdam?"

"Yes, my lord, and a little farther north — as far as Brandon's Camp."

"Then just take that map — give it him, Haldane — and describe for us the nature of the country west of Fishdam Ford. It's high ground, isn't it? A sort of spine? Sumter is lying in that neighborhood, as you probably know. If you don't, it is the fact, and we propose, all being well, to surprise him to-night."

"To-morrow night, by your leave, my lord," some one interjected.

"To-night," Rawdon replied dryly and with

emphasis; and he withered the interrupter with a look. "That is a detail," he continued, "which I confess I have kept from you, gentlemen, — with the exception of the Brigadier and Major Wemyss — until this moment. A mounted force of the 63rd has gone forward, and should be already beyond Mobley Meeting-house. Major Wemyss who is to command them rides express from here within the hour. The attack will be made to-night, or in the small hours of the morning, but it entirely depends for its success on surprise. Our numbers are not large and General Sumter is in some strength, with reinforcements not far off — Triggs, Clarke, and their irregulars. If he has warning he may turn the tables on us. That being so, gentlemen, and because so many of our plans have been disclosed of late — God knows how! — I have advanced the time of the attack to to-night."

There was a general murmur of assent and approval.

"Now, Major Craven," my lord continued, "will you detail for us the nature of the country as you remember it, and as precisely as you can. We have other information, of course, but I wish to see if it tallies with yours. Your return to-day is a piece of good fortune."

I explained with the map before me the main

features, as I remembered them. My former journey had been made at some risk just before Gates's advance to Camden and with a view to an advance on our side. What I detailed seemed to confirm the information already in our possession as well as the report of Sumter's position. Wemyss, who was naturally the most deeply concerned, and who followed my explanation with great care on another map, put a number of questions to me; and in this he was seconded by Webster. When I had answered these questions to the best of my power, Wemyss addressed the man on my right — the same who had risen and sat down again.

I should explain that Webster, the Brigadier, was on my left hand, sitting at the end of the table. I could apprehend by this time who were there. There were seven altogether, five soldiers and two civilians.

"What I want to know is this, Mr. Burton," Wemyss asked. "Are you sure that Triggs and Clarke, with the southern rebels, have not joined Sumter? This is a point of the utmost importance. It is life or death to us. Are you clear about it?"

"Yes, Mr. Burton, let us hear you on that," my lord said.

The question was put at an unlucky moment for my neighbor had just taken a pinch of snuff which set him sneezing. With difficulty he managed to say that — tishoo! on that point he was — tishoo! clear — quite clear, my lord!

"And just one point more, my lord," Wemyss insisted. "Are you sure, Mr. Burton, that Triggs and Clarke are not near enough to join Sumter to-day? Before the time of my attack, sir, do you see? Because that is just as important."

"Yes, we want no more mistakes," my lord chimed in. "Let us be certain this time. What do you say to that, Mr. Burton?"

Mr. Burton, a stoutish man in brown, with a neat well-floured head — I could see so much of him, but little more, as he was next to me — sneezed again and violently. It was all he could do to answer in a half-strangled voice that — 'tishoo! he was sure of that also — quite sure, my lord!

One or two laughed at his predicament, but my lord was not pleased. "If you can't take snuff without sneezing," he said sharply, "why, the devil, man, do you take it! Why do you take it? Now, Wemyss, have you all the information you need, do you think? Are you sure? Don't be hurried. You must not let Sumter get the better of you, as Marion did."

I think that Wemyss was not well pleased with the reminder that he had not been lucky on the Pee Dee.

At any rate he did not take the hint to ask further questions. He was already on his feet and he answered that he thought that he now had all that he wanted. "If I don't do it with what I know," he continued rather sulkily, "I shall not do it at all. And by your leave, my lord," he continued, moving towards the door, "I will lose no more time. My horses are outside and it will be as much as I can do to overtake my men. We can't go by the cross-cuts and wood-roads that these d — d fellows use."

"Nor by the marshes," some one said, hinting slyly at his Pee Dee campaign.

"No, we are not web-footed," Wemyss grunted.

"Well, very good," my lord answered indulgently. "Go, by all means, and good luck to you, Wemyss. Catch that d — d fellow Sumter if you can! By G — d, I hope you may, and good luck to you!"

We echoed the wish, one after another. My lord rose from the table, others rose. There was a little confusion. I turned to say a word to my snuff-taking neighbor, but he had turned his shoulder towards me and was already on his feet, speaking to Haldane, the General's aide, who was between him and the door.

Webster saw that I looked at him. He winked.

"A good man that," he said in a low voice. "He has given us a great deal of information, a vast lot of information. He comes from the other side of the hills on the Tennessee slope. He is a back-waters man, but he knows this country well. A strong King's man and damned useful to us of late, d — d useful, I can tell you."

"If he comes from the Tennessee slope," I said pricking up my ears, "he may know the place I was at. It's on this side, but not far from the foot of the mountains. The man's name was Wilmer — the man who took me. He treated me well, too, General, very well! Shall we ask him?"

Webster was still in his seat at the table — a stout heavy man, slow in his movements, but shrewd and a very able soldier. He raised his voice. "Mr. Burton!" he cried. "Hie! I want you."

But Burton was now within a pace or two of the door. He did not hear, and would have escaped if he had not been forced to give place to the Chief who was in the act of passing out at that moment. This detained Burton, but for an instant only — he seemed to be in a great hurry; and seeing this and that in another moment he would be gone, Webster appealed to Haldane who was also going out.

"Haldane!" he cried. "Stop Mr. Burton! I

157

want to speak to him. Damme, has the man turned deaf all in a minute! What has come to him? Here, bring him back!"

The aide did as he was told, tapping his man on the shoulder, and pointing to us.

"The Brigadier wants you," he said. "He's speaking to you."

"D — n the man, he's as deaf as a post! Mr. Burton!" Webster cried. "Mr. Burton! One minute! Didn't you hear me call you? Major Craven wants to ask you a question."

Webster rose as he spoke. I rose. My lord had disappeared, but could still be heard in the passage speaking to some one. There were only Webster and I, Haldane and Burton left in the room. The civilian, thus summoned — and Webster's voice had grown peremptory — turned back to us; a big clumsy figure of a man with his head sunk low between his shoulders, an enormous stock, and a thick queue. He looked more like a quaker than a planter, and he seemed to be an inveterate snuffer, for in the act of turning he had his box out again and a pinch raised to his nose. A heavy, good-natured-looking man he seemed; one who might have stepped out of a counting-house in 'Change Alley, and whose appearance would have surprised me more if I had not seen the queer wigs and queues in

158

which the New Hampshire farmers, even in the backwoods, took the field.

"Your servant, sir," he said, civilly enough, now we had got him.

"You come from the Tennessee slope, Mr. Burton, I understand?" I said.

"There or thereabouts, sir," he answered in the same tone. And he blew out his cheeks after a clownish fashion.

"Do you know by any chance the man who took me?" I asked. "His plantation lies about four miles east of King's Mountain and just over the colony line. It's on Crowder's creek or one of the small creeks west of the Catawba. They call the place the Bluff and it cannot be very far west of Wahub's Plantation?"

He pondered, a pinch of snuff at his nose. "Well, I am not sure, sir," he said slowly, "I think I should know it."

"His name is Wilmer."

"Wilmer? Wilmer?" he muttered. "Umph?"

"A tall, lean man," I said, thinking to assist his memory, which, it was plain, worked sluggishly. "I should say a man of some standing in his district. He treated me well. He could not have treated me better or behaved more handsomely, indeed. In fact, I may say that he saved my life —"

159

I stopped. I stared at the man, at his short wide face, which would have been jovial if it had not been so heavy, at his powdered head. His fingers, raised to convey the pinch of snuff to his nose covered the lower part of his countenance, but I noted that he had a shaky hand — some of the snuff fell on his stock. He puffed out his cheeks as he prepared to answer, but when he did so, it was only to repeat my last words. "Saved your life, sir, did he?" he murmured. "So I have heard. He took you into his house, I understand?"

I stared at him. "That was so," I said. Where had I seen some one — some one? My heart began to beat quickly.

He sneezed. "Of Wilmer's Bluff?" he muttered. "Well, I think I should know him, Major, I b'lieve I know him. And he saved your life, sir, did he? He saved your life?"

We stared at one another. Haldane, summoned by a voice from the passage turned to leave the room. Webster laughed — evidently the man's oddities were known to him and he saw nothing out of the common in his manner. "Gad, Craven! You look surprised," he said with a chuckle. "But Mr. Burton has a vast deal of information. He knows what is passing as well as any man, by Gad! Well, I must be going. See you at dinner? You had better be going soon, for the Chief is coming back. and he likes to have the room to himself."

Sharp as the shock had been, the moment of time that Webster's words gained for me, helped me to collect myself. Before he was out of the room I spoke. "Yes, Mr. Burton," I said, "we had better be going!"

His eyes questioned me.

"We'll go to my quarters — in the first place," I said.

He had still a hope I think that I had no more than suspicion in my mind — that I did not know; for he fenced with me, his eyes on my face. "In an hour, sir," he said, "I can be at your service. Heartily at your service, sir."

"In an hour," I replied gravely, "it will be too late for either of us to be of service to the other. You know many things, Mr. Burton," I continued, "but I know one thing. You will be wise to give me your arm and to come with me to my quarters at once. Will you go before me?"

I made way for him and followed him closely from the room and the house. Outside I saw Paton seated on one of the benches before the door. "Paton," I said, "come with me. I want you."

My tone surprised him, and reinforced by a glance at my face put him on the alert. He rose at once and joined us. By this time I had a pretty good notion what I should do, and when we had walked a few yards in silence, "Paton," I said, "Mr. Burton is going to give me some information and we want no listeners and no interruption. I am going to take him to our quarters and I want you to keep the door below and to see that no one comes in or goes out while we are together. Do you understand?"

Paton looked at me and looked at Burton and no doubt he saw that the thing, whatever it was, was serious. He whistled softly. "I understand!" he said. And then, "There is my man," he added, "would you like him too?"

"Yes, I would," I said. "Bid him be within call."

Burton maintained an easy silence as he moved beside me, and in this fashion, followed by Paton's man who had fallen in at a sign from his master, we walked up the village street, threading the motley crowd of blacks and whites who thronged it. Soldiers, leaning against garden fences or lounging under the trees, saluted us as we passed. Sutlers' carts went by in a long train. In an interval between two houses the drums were practicing. Here an awkward squad was at drill under a rough-tongued sergeant, whose cane was seldom idle, there a troop of the 14th Dragoons were drawn up awaiting their officer. A shower had fallen earlier in the day, but the sun had shone out and the lively scene, the white frame-houses, the bowering foliage around them, the bright uniforms, the movement, formed one of the cheerful interludes of war.

In other eyes than mine. For my part I walked through it, execrating, bitterly execrating it all — the sunshine, the leaves just touched by autumn, the fleecy sky — all! And fate. The mockery of it and the irony of it, overcame me. Of what moment are the bright hues of the trap to the wild creature that is caught in it?

However, lamentations must wait for another season. I had but a few moments, and I must act, not think. A very short walk brought us to Paton's house in which he had secured for me the sole use of a tiny attic, the only room above stairs in what was but a small cottage. On the threshold I turned to him. "You will keep the door," I said. "No one is to be allowed to go in or out, Paton, until you see me. You understand? Has your man his side-arms?"

Paton looked askance at my companion. "I understand," he said. "You may depend upon me, Major."

"Now, Mr. Burton," I said. "I will follow you, if you please. I think that we can soon despatch this matter."

163

We went in. I pointed to the narrow staircase — it was little better than a ladder — and he went up before me. The room was a mere cock-loft lighted by a tiny square window on the level of my knee and looking to the rear. But it was private and we could just stand upright in the middle of the floor. I closed the door, and turned to him.

CHAPTER IX

THE COURT IS CLOSED

As I was walking all alane
I heard twa corbies making a mane
The tane unto the tither say:
' Where sall we gang and dine to-day?'

' Ye'll sit on his white hause-bane
And I'll pick out his bonnie blue een,
Wi' ae lock o' his gowden hair
We'll theek our nest when it grows bare.'
ANON.

"We had better speak low, Mr. Burton," I said.
"I will be as short as I can. You know the position
as well as I do, and that if I do my duty the result
will be a long rope and a short shrift before night."

He looked about him, and drawing forward his
ample skirts, he took with much calmness — but
I suspected that he was not as cool as he looked —
a seat on my bed. "Have you not made a mistake,
Major?" he drawled.

"No," I answered. "I have made no mistake,
I understand many things now that were dark to me
before; what your daughter feared, and why she
kept you apart from me, and — and the enemy's
knowledge of our plans, Mr. Burton."

He shrugged his shoulders, and made no farther attempt to baffle me or to deny his identity. He sat, a little hunched up on the low bed with his hands in his pockets; and he looked at me, quizzically. Certainly, he was a man of great courage. "Well," he said, "we're in trouble, sir. It has come to that. Poor Con always said that it would, and that if I took you in I should pay for it. Good Lord, if she saw us now! But, as it turns out, the shoe is on the other foot, Major. It is you who will have to pay for it. I saved your life, and you cannot give me up. You cannot do it, my friend!"

I confess that his answer and his impudence confounded me and roused in me an anger which I could hardly control. How I execrated alike the ill luck that had brought my rescuers to the Bluff and the impulse that had led them to wait for a last stirrup-cup — and so to find me! How above all I cursed the chance that had put it into the Chief's head to seek my advice that morning — that morning of all mornings — before the news of my return had gone abroad!

Even for the man before me I was concerned; he had saved my life, he had treated me well, and he had done both in the face of strong temptation to do otherwise. But I was not so much concerned for him as for Constantia. Poor Constantia! The

picture that rose before me, of the girl, of her love
for her father, of her anxiety, of the Bluff, of all,
rent my heart.

"How long have you been doing this?" I asked
harshly. My voice sounded in my own ears like
another man's.

He raised his eyebrows. He did not answer.
He left the burden on me.

"You won't say anything?"

"Only that I saved your life, Major," he replied
quaintly. "I've done my stint, it is for you to do
yours. You can't give me up."

He leaned back, his hands clasped about his knees,
his eyes smiling. Apparently he experienced no
doubt, no anxiety, no alarm; only some faint amusement. But probably behind the mask, which prac-
tice had made to sit easily on him, fear was working
as in other men; probably he felt the halter not far
from his neck. For when I did not answer, "You've
not brought me here for nothing, I suppose?" he
said, speaking in a sharper tone.

I had no difficulty in finding an answer to that.
"No," I said with the bitterness I had so far re-
pressed. "No, if you must know, I have brought you
here, to sink myself something lower than you! To
pay the bill which I owe for my life with my honor!
Oh, its a damned fine pass, sir, you've brought me

167

to!" I continued savagely. "To soil hands that I've kept clean so far, and dirty a name —"

"Stop!" he cried. He was on his feet in a moment, a changed man, sharp, eager, angry. "Lower than me, you say? By G — d, let there be no mistake, Major! If you think I'm ashamed of the work I am doing, I am not! And I'll not let it be said that I am! I am proud of it! I am doing work that not one in ten thousand could do or dare do. Plenty will shoot off guns and face death in hot blood — it's a boy's task. But to face death in cold blood, and daily and hourly without rest or respite; to know that the halter may enter with every man who comes into the room, with every letter that is laid on the table, with a dropped word or a careless look. To know that it's waiting for you outside every house you leave. To face that, day and night, week in week out — that needs nerve! That calls for courage, I say it, sir, who know! And what is the upshot?" He swelled himself out. "Where others strike blows, I win battles!"

"Ay," I cried — he had more to say, had I let him go on — "but sometimes you lose, and this time you have lost. And having lost, you look to me to pay! You look to me, sir! You take the honor, . d — n you, and you leave me the dishonor! But by G — d, if it were not for your daughter, —"

"Ah!" he said, low-voiced and attentive.

"You should pay your losings this time, though you saved my life twice over!"

"Oh, oh!" he said in the same low voice. He sat back on the bed again, and stared at me, as if he saw a different man before him. After a pause, "Well," he said, "I was a fool, Major, to blow my trumpet, and ruffle your temper. If I wanted to put my head in your folks' noose, that was the way to do it. But every mother dotes on her own booby. Well, you'll hear no more singing from me. I'm silent!"

"When I think," I cried, "of your boasts of what you have done!"

"Don't think of them," he answered. "Set me dawn for a fool, Major, and let it rest there. Or think of the Bluff and Con. She's a good girl, and fond of her father and — well, you know how it is with us."

I was able to collect myself within a minute or two, and — "Mark me," I said firmly, "I will give you up, Wilmer, I will give you up still, if you depart one jot from what I tell you. You will remain in this room for twenty-four hours. By that time Major Wemyss will have done his work, and as the time of the attack has been advanced by a night, what you may have communicated to your people should not change the issue. To-morrow I will release you, and give you two hours start. You will be wise to avail yourself of it, for at the end of that time I shall see Lord Rawdon, make a clean breast of it, and take the consequences. I shall be dismissed, and if I get my deserts I shall be shot; in any case my name will be disgraced. But if I am not to give you up, there is no other way out of the pit in which you have caught me."

He thought for a moment. Then "I will give you," he said, "my word if you like, Craven, not to pass on any more —"

"What, a spy's word?" I cried — and very foolish it was of me to say it. But the man had brought so much evil on me that I longed to wound him. "No! I'll have no truck with you and no bargain, Captain Wilmer. It shall be as I have said, exactly as I have said," I repeated, " or I call in the nearest guard. That is plain speaking."

He shrugged his shoulders. "As you please, my friend," he said. "But why not open Rawdon's eyes as to me — when I'm gone? and say no more?"

"And leave myself in your power?" I cried. "No! I tell you I will make no bargain with you and have no truck! That way traitors are made!"

"I will swear if you like, Major — "

"No," I replied angrily, "if I do this, I will pay for it."

He shrugged his shoulders once more. "Well! it's your difficulty," he said dryly, relapsing into his earlier manner. "And it is for you to get out of it."

"Yes," I said, "and I shall get out of it in my own way and on my own terms."

He did not answer and I turned to go, but I cast my eyes round the place, before I left him. A glance was enough to assure me that a man of his size could not pass through the window, while there was no other way from the room except through the guarded door. I went down to Paton. I must secure his help for I had still something to do.

Naturally a lively soul, he was agog with curiosity, which the trouble in my face did not lessen. "What is the trouble, Major?" he asked, taking my arm, and drawing me apart. "And where's old Snuff and Sneeze?"

"He's in my room and he's going to stay there," I said. Then I told him a part of the truth; that I had a clue to a spy, a man in the camp at this moment. I added that I believed Burton also knew the man and might be tempted to warn him, if he were free to do so. That if Burton attempted to leave the house, therefore, he must be arrested; but that I aimed at avoiding this if possible, as I did not wish to estrange the man. "I leave you on guard," I said. "I depend on you, Paton."

"But I'm on duty, Major," he objected, "in an hour."

"I shall be back in half an hour," I explained. "After that I will be answerable."

"Very good," he rejoined. "But you know what you are doing? You have no doubt I suppose? Burton has the Chief's ear, and Webster believes in him and makes much of him. There'll be the deuce of a fracas if he's arrested and there's nothing in it."

"Do you arrest him if he leaves the house," I said, "and leave it to me to explain. I don't think he will, and as long as he remains upstairs let him be. That's clear, is it not?"

He allowed that it was, and with a heavy heart I left him in charge and went on my errand.

I suppose that there were the same splashes of red among the trees, where the King's uniform peeped through the foliage, the same men lounging about, the same squads practicing the Norfolk discipline, the same rack of thin clouds passing across the sunshine, the same drum playing the Retreat and the Tattoo, or the plaintive notes of Roslyn Castle. But I neither saw nor heard any of these things. My whole mind was bent on finding my lord and getting an express — no matter on what excuse — sent after Wemyss to warn him, and to put him on his guard. An orderly on a swift horse might still by hard riding overtake him; and such a message as "the enemy expect you to-morrow night, but do not expect you to-night — have a care" might avail. At worst it would relieve my conscience, at the same time that it lessened the heavy weight of responsibility that crushed me.

I should then have done all that I could, and nearly all that could be done, were the truth known.

But my lord was not at Headquarters, nor could they say where he was; and when I sought Webster, who had his lodgings at a tavern, a hundred yards farther down the road, he, too, was away. He had gone to visit the outposts eastward. Time was passing, Wemyss had a start of two hours, and was himself riding express; every moment that I lost made it more doubtful if he could be overtaken. With a groan I gave up the idea, and, turning about, I made the best of my way back towards Paton's quarters.

Fifty yards short of the house whom should I meet but Haybittle, red-faced, grey-haired, and dogged, his green uniform shabby with hard usage. He was riding up the street with an orderly behind him, and when he saw me, he pulled his horse across the road and hailed me with a grin. "Major," he said, "What's this? There's a young woman of the name of Simms hunting you like a wild cat. It's easy to see what it is she has against you! Come, I didn't think it of you — really I didn't, Major! A man of your —"

"Pooh!" I cried, "it's her husband that she wishes to hear of."

"Oh, of course, it's always the husband is the trouble!" he laughed. "You are right there!"

"Well, come on," I answered irritably, "I want to hear about the woman, but I cannot stop now. Come to Paton's and tell me what she said. He's waiting for me, and he's next for duty. I am late as it is!"

I pushed on, and Haybittle turned his horse and followed at my heels. Over my shoulder, "I wish you'd seen that Quaker fellow, Burton, a minute ago," he·said. "Lord, he was a figure, Major! He'd borrowed a troop-horse, he told me, and it had tripped over a tent-rope in the lines and given him a fall. His stock was torn —"

I turned on the man so sharply, that his horse had much ado not to knock me down. "What?" I cried. "You met Burton — now?"

"Two minutes ago. He was riding express for —"

"Riding?"

"To be sure, riding towards Mobley's Meeting House, and sharp, too! Why, what is it, man? You look as if you had seen a bailiff!"

THE COURT IS CLOSED

I did not doubt. In a moment I knew. Though the house stood only twenty paces from us and Paton was at the door, I did not go in to see. A wave of anger, fierce, unreasoning, irresistible swept me away — and yet had I reasoned what else could I have done? I seized Haybittle's rein with my free hand. "Then follow him!" I cried, pointing the way with my crippled arm. "After him! Ride like fury, man! He's a spy! After him! Stop him, or shoot him!"

Haybittle stared at me as if I had gone mad. "Do you mean it?" he asked. "Are you sure, Major? Quite sure?" He held his cane suspended in the air.

"Go, man, go!" I cried, wildly excited. "My order! Follow him, follow him! Fishdam is his point! Turn all after him that you meet. A spy! Shout it before you as you go!"

"A spy?" Haybittle yelled. "D — n him, we'll catch him!" His cane fell, his horse leapt off at a gallop. The orderly followed, his knee abreast of the Captain's crupper. Two troopers of the Fourteenth who were passing, heard the cry, turned their horses, and spurred after them. With a loud View Halloo the four pounded away down the road, spreading the alarm before them, as they rode.

Paton who had heard what was said rushed int

175

the house. He did not believe it, I think. In a trice he was out again. "I can't open the door," he panted. "The bed is against it. Round the house, Major!"

He led the way, we ran round the house. At the back the little window, ten feet from the ground, was open. Below it a plot of rough orchard ground, in which two or three trees had been felled, ran down to a branch. On the farther side of the water were some horse lines. We stared up at the window. "But, d — mme, man, he couldn't do it!" Paton cried. "He couldn't pass. Burton is as fat as butter!"

I swore. "That's what I forgot!" I said. "He's padded! He's as lean as a herring!"

We ran round to the front again. The hallooing came faintly up the road. Already all the camp in that direction was roused and in a ferment. Two troopers galloped by us as we reached the road. An officer followed, spurring furiously. "That's Swanton on the bay that won the match last week," Paton said; and he yelled "Forrard away! After him! If Burton is on a common troop-horse," he continued, "and he cannot have had time to pick and choose, his start won't save him! The bay will be at his girths within five miles!"

"If they are to catch him they must do it quickly,"

I groaned. "If he draws clear of the settlement, he knows the roads and they don't."

"He'll be afraid to extend his horse until the alarm overtakes him," Paton answered. "He would be stopped if he did, and questioned. There are many on the roads this morning. Haybittle noticed him, you see. But what does it all mean, Craven?" he continued.

We were standing, looking down the road. Half a hundred others, all staring the same way, were grouped about us. "He's gone to warn Sumter," I said dully. The excitement was dying down in me and I was beginning to see what lay before me — whether he escaped or were taken. "If he reaches Sumter before Wemyss attacks — and Wemyss may not attack before daybreak — heaven help us! The surprise will be on the wrong side!"

Paton whistled. "Our poor lads!" he said.

For a moment my anger rose anew. But, Paton looking curiously at me and wondering, I don't doubt, why I had given the man the chance to escape, my heart sank again. Wilmer's determined act, his grim persistence in his damnable mission, had sunk me below anything I had foreseen. If he escaped, the blood of our men lay on my conscience. If he were taken, I had bargained with him to no purpose, and soiled my hands to no end. My act must send him to the gallows, my very voice must witness against him! And Con? Ay, poor Con, indeed, I thought. For even as I stood stricken and miserable, gazing with scores of sight-seers down the road, and waiting for the first news of the issue, she rose before my mind's eye, tall and slender and grave and dressed in white, as I had seen her on that evening, when she had flung herself into her father's arms; the father whom I, then crouching in pain in the saddle below, was destined to bring to this! To bring to this! I thought with horror of my arrival at the Bluff, of the lights, the barking dogs, the blacks' grinning faces and staring eyeballs! I thought with terror of her cry that ill would come of it — ill would come of it! I felt myself the blind tool of fate working out a tragedy, which had begun beside poor Simms's body in that little clearing fringed with the red sumach bushes!

Why, oh why had not the man been content to stay where I had placed him? And why, oh why — I saw the error now — had I not taken the parole he had offered me? I did not doubt that he would have kept it, if I had trusted him. But I had refused it, and the chance of striking a new and final blow had tempted him to my undoing.

So different were my thoughts from the unconscious Paton's, as shoulder to shoulder we stared down the road; while round us the crowd grew dense and men of the 23rd tossed questions from one to the other, and troopers of the Legion coming up from Headquarters drew bridle to learn what was on foot — until presently their numbers blocked the road. Bare-armed men, still rubbing bit or lock, made wagers on the result, and peered into the distance for the first flutter of news. A spy? Men swore grimly. "Hell! I hope they catch him!" they growled.

Presently into the thick of this crowd there rode up the Brigadier, asking with objurgations what the men meant by blocking the road. The nearest to him gave ground, those farther away explained. One or two pointed to me. He pushed his horse through the throng to my side.

"What's this rubbish they are telling me?" he exclaimed peevishly. "Burton, man? A spy? It's impossible! You can't be in earnest?"

"Yes, sir," I said sorrowfully; and I knew that with those words I cast the die. "He was fighting against us at King's Mountain. He is disguised, but I knew the man — after a time."

"His name is not Burton?"

"No, sir," I said. "His name is Wilmer."

"What? The man who — " he stopped. He looked oddly at me, and raised his eyebrows. My

story was pretty well known in the camp by this
time. Paton had spread it. "Why, the very man
that you —"

"Yes, sir," I said. "The man who captured me
— and treated me well."

"Well, I am d — d! But there, I hope to God
they take him, all the same! Why he's known everything, shared in everything, sat at our very tables!
Not a loyalist has been trusted farther, or known
more! He must have cost us hundreds of our poor
fellows, if this be true. He's —"

"He's a brave man, General," I said. speaking on
I know not what impulse.

"And he'll look very well on a rope!" Webster
retorted. "Still, Craven, I'm sorry for you."

I could say nothing to that, and a few moments
later an end was put to our suspense. A man came
into sight far down the road, galloping towards us.
As he drew nearer I saw that it was a sutler on a
wretched nag. He waved a rag above his head, a
signal which was greeted by the crowd with a volley
of cheers and cries. "They've caught him! Hurrah!
They've caught him!" a score of voices shouted.

I could not speak. Alike the tragedy of it, and
the pity of it took me by the throat, and choked me.
I could have sworn at the heedless jeering crowd,
I could have spat curses at them. I waited only

until another man came up and confirmed the news. Then I went into the house and hid myself.

Afterwards I learned that the horse which Wilmer had seized was a sorry beast incapable of a gallop and well-known in the troop. Viewed before he had gone a mile, and aware that he was out-paced, the fugitive had turned off the road, hoping to hide in the woods. But to do this he had had to face his horse at a ditch, and the brute instead of leaping it, had bundled into it. Before Wilmer could free himself or rise from the ground his pursuers had come up with him.

I have said that I went into the house and hid myself. Poor Con! The girl's face rose before me, and dragged at my heartstrings. I saw her, as I had seen her many times, bending her dark head over the spinning-wheel, while the pigeons pecked about her feet, and the cattle came lowing through the ford, and round the home pastures and the quiet homestead stretched the encircling woods, and the misty hills; and I turned my face to the wall and I wished that I had never been born! My poor Con!

*   *   *   *   *

Owing to my lord's absence from the camp during the greater part of the day a court for the trial of the prisoner could not be assembled until four in the afternoon. I dare not describe what those intervening hours were to me, how long, how miserable, how cruelly armed with remorse and upbraidings! Nor will I say much of the trial. The result from the first was certain; there was no defence and there was other evidence than mine. Since his disguise had been taken from him two men in the camp, one a Tory from the Waxhaws, the other a deserter, had recognized the prisoner; and for a time I hoped that the Court, having a complete case, would dispense with my presence. My position, and the fact that he had spared my life and sheltered me in his house had become generally known, and many felt for me. But the laws of discipline are strict, and duty, when the lives of men hang upon its performance, is harshly interpreted. The Court saw no reason why I should be spared. At any rate they did not spare me.

When the time to enter came I was possessed by a sharp fear of one moment — the moment when I should meet Wilmer's eyes. They had taken his stuffed clothes from him and brushed the powder from his hair, and when I entered he stood between his guards, a lean, straight sinewy Southerner, very like the man who had stood over me with a Deckhard in the little clearing. The light fell on his face, and he was smiling. Whatever of inward quailing, whatever of the natural human shrinking from the approach of death he felt, he masked to perfection. As for the moment I had so much feared, it was over before I was aware.

"Hello, Major!" he said, and he nodded to me pleasantly. I don't know what my face showed, but he nodded again, as if he would have me know that all was well with him and that he bore me no malice. "You want another sup of whisky, Major," he cried genially.

"I need hardly ask you after that," the President said, clasping his hands about the hilt of the sword which stood between his knees, "if you know the prisoner?"

"I do, sir."

"Tell your story, witness."

The sharp, business-like tone steadied me, helped me. With a calmness that surprised myself I stated that the prisoner before the Court, who passed in Camp, and in disguise, under the name of Burton, was the same man who under the name of Wilmer had fought against us at King's Mountain, and had there taken me when wounded, and cared for me in his own house.

"You were present," the President asked, "when the plans for Major Wemyss's advance were discussed at Headquarters before my Lord Rawdon?"

"I was, sir."

"Was the prisoner also there?"

"He was, sir."

"In disguise and under a false name?"

I bowed.

"He was taking part in the debate as one knowing the district?"

"He was."

"You recognize the prisoner beyond a shadow of a doubt?"

"I do."

Had the prisoner any questions to ask the witness? He shrugged his shoulders and smiled. No, he had none. Other formalities followed — curt, decent, all in order. A stranger coming in, ignorant of the issue, would have thought that the matter at stake was trivial. The President's eye was already collecting the votes of the other members of the Court, when I intervened. I stood forward. I desired to say something.

"Be short, sir. On what point?"

The prisoner's admirable and humane conduct to me, which by preserving my life had directly wrought his undoing. I desired some delay, and a reference to Lord Cornwallis —

"The matter is irrelevant to the charge," the President said, stopping me harshly. "You can stand back, sir. Stand back!"

THE COURT IS CLOSED

Finding — guilty. Sentence — in the usual form. Execution — within twenty-four hours. All subject to confirmation by the acting Commander-in-Chief.

"The Court is closed."

I have but sketched the scene, having no heart for more and no wish to linger over it. There are hours so painful and situations so humiliating that the memory shrinks from traversing the old ground. Wilmer, on his side, had no ground for hope, and so could bear himself bravely and with an effort could add magnanimity to courage. He could smile on me, call me "Major" in the old tone, banter me grimly. But my part was harder. To meet his eyes, aware of the return I had made; to know that I, whose life he had saved and whom he had taken to his home, had doomed him to an ignominious death; to shrink from the compassionate looks of friends and the curious gaze of those who scented a new sensation and enjoyed it; and as a background to all this to see in fancy the ashen face and woful eyes of the girl I loved and had orphaned, the girl who far away in that peaceful scene knew nothing of what was passing here — with all this was it wonderful that when I went back to my quarters Paton refused to leave me?

"No, I am not going," he said. "You are too near the rocks, Major! It's no good looking at me

185

as if you could kill me. I brought you away from that place, I know, and I'm d — d sorry that I did! When you are next taken you may rot in Continental dungeons till the end of time for me! I'll not interfere I warrant you. I've had my lesson. All the same, Major, listen! You're taking this too hardly. It's no fault of yours. The man himself doesn't blame you. He had his chance. He knew the stake, he went double or quits, and he lost; and he's going to pay. Through you? Well, or through me or through another — what does it matter?"

"And Con? His daughter?" I said. "It's the same to her, I suppose! Oh, it's a jest, a d — d fine jest that fate has played me, isn't it!" And I laughed in his face, scaring him sadly, he told me afterwards.

For two or three minutes he was silent. Then he touched me on the shoulder. "I was afraid of this," he said softly. "See, here, man, you'll be the better for doing something. Go and see my lord. He's a gentleman. Tell him. Tell him all. See him before he goes out in the morning — he will be dining now. I excused you, of course. I don't think he'll grant your request; frankly I don't think he dare grant it — it's a flagrant case! But you will be doing something!"

I agreed, miserably, because there was nothing

else I could do. But I had no hope of the result. And the slow and wretched hours went by while I walked the room in a fever of suspense, and Paton in spite of my angry remonstrances stayed with me, sometimes poring over a soldier's song-book by the light of the single candle, and at others going down for a few moments to answer some curious friend. I could not face them myself, and when the first came, I started to my feet. "Don't for God's sake," I cried, "tell them!"

"Lord, no!" he answered. "Do you think I'm an ass, Major? Your arm's the size of my leg — that'll do for them! It's all they'll hear from me!"

The longest night has an end; and mercifully this was not one of the longest. For about midnight, worn out by my feelings and broken by the fatigue of the journey from Rocky Mount, I lay down, and promptly I fell asleep and slept like a log till long after reveillé had sounded, and the camp was astir. The awakening was dreary; but, thank God, I drew strength from the new day. The sharpest agony had passed, I was now master of myself, resigned to the worst and prepared for it. True, I felt myself years older, I saw in life a tragedy. But in my sleep I had risen to the tragic level, and, waking, I knew that it became me to face life with the dignity with which her father was confronting death.

CHAPTER X

THE WOMAN'S PART

You no doubt are acquainted with the great attention and tenderness shown my son at Camden by all the British officers that he has seen, and the Gentlemen of the Faculty, as well as the maternal kindness of Mrs. Clay.

CORRESPONDENCE OF MRS. PINKNEY.

I was at Headquarters soon after nine in the morning. There are joints in the armor of all, the great have their bowels, and I have no doubt that had he told the truth, my lord would have given much to avoid me and my petition. But he did not try to do so, and in the spirit which now inspired me, I recognised the law under which we all lay. He, I, the man who must suffer, all moved in the clutch of remorseless duty, all were forced on by the mind that over-rode the body and its preferences.

Willing or unwilling, he met me with much kindness. "What is it, Craven?" he said. "But I fear, I very much fear that I know your errand."

"If you could see me alone, my lord?" I said.

"Certainly I will." He nodded to Haldane and in a moment we were left together.

188

THE WOMAN'S PART

I told him the story, all the story; and he heard me with sympathy. I have said that he was a man of my age, not yet thirty, but authority had given him force and decision, and the patience that goes with those qualities. "In Lord Cornwallis's absence, it lies with you, my lord," I concluded, when I had told my tale, "to confirm the finding and sentence. The man's life is forfeit, I cannot deny it. I do not attempt to say otherwise. But the circumstances are such — he gave me my life, I am taking his — that I am compelled to put forward my own services and implore on my own account what I cannot ask, my lord, on his. If he were confined in the West Indies, for the duration of the war, or were sent to England — "

He stopped me. "My dear Craven, the thing is impossible," he said gently. "Impossible! You must see that for yourself. In another man's case you would see it. I should be unworthy of command, unworthy of the post I hold, unworthy of the obedience of the men whose lives are in my hands, if I listened to you! Frankly, I could not hold up my head if I did this. And that is not all," he continued in a firmer tone. "I have news, by express this moment. Wemyss's force has been repulsed, badly repulsed near Fishdam. He is wounded and a prisoner. The account that we have is confused,

189

but it is certain that the enemy knew that the attack was coming and awaited it a gunshot behind their campfires; so that when our poor lads ran in they came under a heavy fire from the woods. I have not a doubt, therefore, that this man, Wilmer, had a confederate in the camp, and short as his time was, contrived to pass on tidings of the change of date."

It was a home blow and I reeled under it. I had had little hope before; I had none now. Still I had made up my mind as to my duty, and I strove afresh to move him. He listened for a moment. Then he cut me short.

"No!" he replied, more curtly, "No! you have no case. The punishment of a spy is known, fixed, unalterable, Craven. It was carried out in the case of Major André, a hard, an extreme case. But it was carried out. This is a flagrant case. You ask an impossibility, man, and you ought to know it!"

"Then I will trouble your lordship for one moment only," I said. "I have a duty to the King —, I have discharged it by informing against Captain Wilmer; I have discharged it at great cost to myself. But I have a duty, also, to the man who saved my life at the price, as it has turned out, of his own! That duty I have not discharged until I have done all that it is in my power to do to save him. May

I remind your lordship that my father has supported the government steadily and consistently in the House with two votes, and has never sought a return in place or pension. Were he here, I will answer for it, that he would not only indorse the request I make that this man's life be spared, but that he would consider its allowance a full return for all his services in the past."

"And, by God!" Rawdon replied, striking the table with his hand, "I would not grant that request, no, not if Lord North himself endorsed it, Major Craven. In his Excellency's absence I command here, mine is the responsibility! I will not make that responsibility immeasurably more heavy, sir, by stooping to a weakness which must rob me, and rightly rob me, of the confidence of every soldier in the camp. I should deserve to be shot, if I did so! There, I have been patient, Craven — I have been patient because I know your position. I have given you a good hearing, but I can hear no more. The thing you ask is impossible. The man must suffer."

"Then, my lord," I replied, "I am compelled to take the only other step open to me. Since neither my own services nor my father's are thought to be sufficient to entitle me to a thing which I have so much at heart, I beg leave to resign his Majesty's commission. Here is my sword, my lord, and I no longer consider myself — "

"Stop!" he replied. "This is nonsense. D—d nonsense!" he continued angrily, "I'll not allow you to resign. Take up your sword, Major Craven, or by G—d, I'll put you under arrest!"

"You can do that, my lord," I said, "if you please. I, for my part believe that I am only doing what honor requires of me." And I turned on my heel, and, though he called me back, I went straight out of the room leaving my sword on the table. I believe the act was irregular, but it was the only way in which I could bear witness to the strength of my feelings.

I had taken in doing this what many would consider a foolish step; but I knew, too, that nothing short of this would acquit me in my own mind; and as I left the house I was at no pains to defend the step to myself. Haldane and the others, who were sitting under the trees before the door, looked at me as I came out, but taking the hint from my face, they let me pass without speech. Haldane went in immediately, and thinking that he might be ordered to carry out the Chief's threat, I moved away down the street. Not that I cared whether I were placed under arrest or no; I was indifferent. But to remain before the house might be taken for a flouting of authority not in the best taste and beyond what I intended.

I had tried all that I could, and I had failed. There remained only one thing which I could do for Wilmer. I must see him. He might have something to say, some message to leave, some service I could perform at the last. I looked along the village street with its thronged roadway and its neat white houses peeping through foliage that blew to and fro tempestuously. The dust flew, and the flag above Headquarters leapt against its staff, for the morning though it was not cold was windy and overcast. As I looked down the road my eyes stopped at the tavern where Webster had his billet. It was nearly — not quite — opposite the house in which I knew that Wilmer was confined; and as I gazed, thinking somberly of the man whose fate had become bound up with mine, and whose last hours were passing so quickly, I saw a negro, bearing something covered with a cloth, go across the road from the tavern to the house. I guessed that he was taking Wilmer's meal to him and I turned the other way. A later hour would suit my purpose better. We, English, whatever our faults may be, bear little rancor, and I had no doubt that even if I were put under arrest, I should be allowed to see the prisoner.

I passed idly along the street in the direction of Paton's quarters. On either hand were loungers perched on the garden fences or leaning against them. The roadway was crowded with forage wagons driven by negro teamsters, with carts from the country laden with fruit and vegetables, with fatigue-parties passing at the double. Troopers rode by me in the green of the Legion or the blue of the Dragoons and everywhere were watchful natives and grinning blacks and women in sun-bonnets whose eyes little escaped. But my thoughts were elsewhere and my eyes roved over the scene and saw nothing, until my feet had borne me a good part of the way to Paton's.

Then I saw her.

She and a negro were standing beside two horses from which they had just dismounted. A little circle of loiterers and busybodies had gathered round them and were eyeing them curiously and questioning them. The horses, jaded and over-ridden, hung their heads, and blew out their nostrils. The black, scared by his surroundings, glanced fearfully hither and thither — it was clear that he felt himself to be in the enemy's camp. But Constantia showed no sign of fear, or of anything but fatigue. Her eyes travelled gravely round the circle, questioned, challenged, met admiration with pride. And yet — and yet, along with the grief and despair that reigned in her breast — that must have reigned there! — there must have lurked, also, some seed of woman's weakness; for as her eyes, in leaping a gap in the circle, met mine and held them — and held them, so that for a moment I ceased to breathe — I felt her whole soul travel to me in appeal.

One thing was clear to me at once: that as yet she did not know the part I had played. For had she known it, her eyes instead of meeting mine would have shunned me, as if I had been the plague.

And that gave me courage. Heedless for the moment of what might ensue, or of what she must eventually learn, I pushed my way through the men, I uncovered, I reached her side. Then, on a nearer view, I saw the change that sorrow and fatigue had wrought in her. She was white as paper, and against the white her hair hung in black clinging masses on her cheeks. Her eyes shone out of dark circles, and her homespun habit was splashed with the mud of many leagues. With all this, I was able to address her, encouraged by her look, as simply as if I had parted from her an hour before — as if I had expected her and knew her plans. "My quarters are near here," I said. "I will take you to them," I added. That was all.

"Tell him," she answered, with a glance at her

attendant. She spoke as if, with all her courage, she had hardly strength to utter the words.

I did so, and the idlers about us, noting my rank, fell back. The crowd broke up. Tom — it was he — led the horses on. We followed, both silent. Forty yards brought us to the door of Paton's house.

When we were inside, "Will you give me some wine?" she said.

I looked for the wine and as I did so, I was aware of Paton escaping from the room with a face of dismay. He recognized her, of course, but I had other things to do than to think of him. I found some Madeira and filled a large glass and gave it to her. She took a piece of bread from her pocket and ate a mouthful or two with the wine, sitting the while on a box with her eyes fixed on vacancy

I have written down all that she said; and for my part I stood beside her, not venturing a word. The knowledge that she must presently learn all, and in particular must learn that it was I who had done this, I who had put the halter round her father's neck, paralyzed my tongue. When she should have learned all, I could serve her no longer, I could do no more for her. It was not for me that her eyes would then seek, nor from my hand that she would take wine.

She set down the glass. "You will take me to Lord Rawdon," she said.

I don't know whether I had foreseen this; but at any rate I took it as a matter of course and made no demur. I suppose Paton heard her also, wherever he was, for immediately I found him at my elbow. "I'll go on," he muttered in my ear. "I'll arrange it. But it's the devil, it's the very devil!"

He did not explain himself, but I knew that he meant it was hard, cruelly hard on us! As for her, she seemed to be unconscious of his presence.

When he had had five minutes start we set out. Already it had gone abroad who my companion was, as such things will spread in a camp, and a curious crowd stood waiting before the door; a crowd that in the circumstances — for Wemyss's check was no longer a secret — could not but be hostile to Wilmer. But when she appeared, looking so proud and pale and composed — not even the wine had brought the faintest color to her cheeks — it was to the credit of our people that there was not a man who did not stand to attention and salute. Not a gibe or a taunt was heard, and I believe that the looks that followed us as we proceeded along the street, were laden with a rough but understanding pity.

Halfway she spoke to me, looking not at me but steadily to the front. "At what hour," she asked with a shiver which she could not restrain, "is it to be?"

"Four o'clock," I replied.

"And it is now?"

"Ten."

A moment later, "I must see my lord alone," she said.

"Yes, I understand," I replied, and so occupied with the matter was I that, a moment later, unconscious of what I was doing, I met with a stony stare the astonished gaze of the Brigadier, who was riding by and drew to the side of the road as if he made way for a procession. "I will try to arrange it," I continued with dry lips. "I have seen Lord Rawdon this morning. It was useless." Then, "You mustn't hope," I muttered. "Don't!"

She did not answer.

Outside Headquarters officers were loitering in a greater number than usual, drawn thither by the news of Wemyss's defeat. I suppose that Paton had passed the word to them, as he went by, for those who were seated rose as we passed between them. Paton himself stood inside the door, talking urgently to Haldane whom he had taken by the button, and who reflected to perfection his face of dismay.

"This lady is Captain Wilmer's daughter," I

said, as we came up to them. "She desires to see Lord Rawdon."

Haldane seemed to have a difficulty in speaking. When he did, "His lordship will see her," he said, looking not at her but at me. "He considers it to be his duty to do so, if the lady desires it. But I am ordered to say that she must draw no hope from the fact, Major Craven. I am instructed to impress upon her that an interview can do no good. If after that she still desires to see his lordship —"

Constantia bowed her head.

"You understand, Madam?" Haldane persisted. "You still desire it — in face of what I have said?"

She bent her head again. He turned on his heel, opened the door behind him and signed to her to enter the room. Then he closed the door upon her. By common consent we moved away and went outside. "Poor beggar!" Haldane muttered. "I wouldn't be in his shoes at this moment for all his pay and appointments. Hanged if I would!" Then, "Curse the war, I say!"

"I say the same!" Paton replied, and twitching the other's sleeve he drew him aside. They encountered and turned back some men who were moving towards us — I have no doubt to learn what was on foot.

I took my seat on the most remote bench on the left of the door, and apart from the crowd; and I waited. How long? I cannot say. I had no hope that the girl would succeed; I was in no suspense on that account. All my anxiety centered in another matter. When she came out she would have heard all from Rawdon. She would have learned the truth and my part in the story. Between them the facts must come out; they could not be hid. And then she would stand alone, quite alone in this strange camp, with four o'clock before her. How would she survive it? What would become of her? The sweat stood on my brow. I waited — waited, knowing that that must be the end of it.

I felt that I should be aware of her knowledge as soon as I saw her. She would feel by instinct where I had placed myself, and she would turn the other way. Or perhaps she would look at me once, and the horror in her eyes would wither me. So far there had been a strange mingling of sweet and bitter in the confidence which she had placed in me, in the way in which she had turned to me, trusted me, leant on me. But when she came out, knowing all, there would be an end of that.

Unheeding, I watched the traffic of the camp pass before me. I saw Carroll go by, and the officer who had presided at the court-martial. Then Tom, the negro, passed, chattering in the company of two other blacks, one of them a teamster. Apparently he had plucked up courage and had found companions. They went towards the tavern. Next the Provost-Marshal appeared; he came towards us, but was waylaid by Haldane and Paton who entered into a heated argument with him — not far from me but just out of earshot. He seemed hard to persuade about something; he glanced my way, argued, hesitated. Finally he yielded and turned away, flinging a sharp sentence over his shoulder. Paton replied, there was a distant rejoinder. The Marshal disappeared down the road, shrugging his shoulders, as if he disclaimed — something.

A man near me laughed. Another said that Paton would get on.

The latter made an angry answer, looking at me. I did not understand. I was waiting. Would she never come? Was it possible that he was listening to her? That he would —

Here was the Provost-Marshal returning anew. Apparently he had thought better of it, for his face was hard with purpose. But again Haldane and Paton met him. They assailed him, argued with him, almost buffeted him; finally they took him by the arms, turned him about, and marched him off. A ripple of laughter ran along the benches. "As

201

good as a play!" some one said. I did not understand. Surely she must come soon.

Yes, she was coming at last. I caught the tinkle of a hand-bell, the sentry stood at attention, Haldane hurried into the house. I rose.

She came out and, thank God, she did not know. She did not know, for her eyes sought mine, she turned towards me. She even gave me a pitiful shadow of a smile, as if, after wading through deep waters, she saw land ahead. I went to her. The men about us rose and remained standing as we walked away together. She turned in the direction of my quarters.

I did not dare to question her and we had gone some distance before she broke the silence. Then she told me, still looking straight before her and speaking with the same unnatural calm, that Lord Rawdon had respited the sentence for twenty-four hours to enable her to carry an appeal to Lord Cornwallis. But that he had not given her the smallest hope that the sentence would be altered. He had impressed this upon her almost harshly.

"But His Excellency is at Charles Town!" I protested, dumbfounded by this suggestion of the impossible. "You cannot go to Charles Town, and return in twenty-four hours!"

"He is at the Santee High Hills," she answered.

202

Her tone implied that she had known this and had not learned it from Lord Rawdon. Then in a dry hard voice she explained that she was to be allowed to see her father at three o'clock. She would start an hour later.

"For the High Hills?"

"Yes."

"But you will die of fatigue," I cried. "If you are to do this you must rest and eat." I knew that she had ridden sixty miles in the last thirty-six hours and had done it under the stress of intense emotion.

She assented, saying meekly that she would do as I thought best. Then, as we entered, "You will come with me?" she said. And with that she turned to me, and looked at me with something of the old challenge in her eyes, looked as one not asking a favor, so much as demanding a right. Or, if the look did not mean that I was unable to say what it meant, beyond this, that it gave me a sort of shock. It was as if she had shown a different face for a moment. Had she known the truth, then she might have looked at me in such a fashion. But in that case she would not have asked me to go with her, I was sure of that.

Still the look was disturbing, and I hesitated. I reflected that her father would tell her the truth;

that before four o'clock she would learn all. In the meantime, however, I could be of use to her, I could save her from some trials. And so "Certainly I will go," I said, "if you wish it. If you still wish it, when the time comes."

"Thank you," she answered wearily. "I do wish it — and you owe us as much as that."

"I owe you —"

She stopped me, raising her hand. "I cannot take Tom," she continued, "for reasons. And the horses? Will you arrange about them? I am — I am very tired." She turned her back on me, and with a weary sigh she sat down.

I told her that I would do everything and see to everything, and I hastened away to find the woman on whom we were quartered. I had a meal prepared, and Paton's room made ready, and water brought and brushes and soap. To do this, to do anything relieved my pent-up feelings, yet while I went about the task, the look that she had given me, when she had asked me to go with her, haunted me. What did it mean? It had impressed itself unpleasantly upon me as at variance with the rest of her conduct, with her confidence, her docility, her dependence on me. For in other matters she had turned to me as a helpless child might turn; and though her acts proved that she had a course of action marked out, and was following that course, her manner would have appealed to a heart of stone.

Presently I was aware of Paton looking in to the room with the same scared face. He beckoned me to him. "You will want horses, won't you?" he whispered.

"Yes," I said.

"How many?"

"Two," I said. "Good ones."

"I'll arrange it," he answered. "Leave it to me and stay where you are. At what time?"

"Four," I said.

He went away. The next to appear was Tom, who talked with his mistress for some minutes while I was above stairs, making ready for the journey. Presently he departed. By that time the hasty meal I had ordered was laid and I induced her to sit down to it, while I waited on her. Need I say that then, more than ever, the strangeness of the relations between us came home to me? That she should be here, in my room, in my care, eating an ordinary meal while I attended on her, handed her this or that, and caught now and again the sad smile with which she thanked me — could anything exceed the marvel of it? Her trust in me, the intimacy of it, the silence — for she rarely spoke — all increased the air of unreality; an unreality so great that when the meal was finished and she went to Paton's room to lie down and rest, it had scarcely seemed out of the question had I gone in with her, covered her, and tucked her up!

After that, through three hours of stillness and silence I kept guard in the outer room, staring at the door behind which she lay; and love and pity choked me, and swelled my heart to bursting. How was she suffering! How was she doomed to suffer! What a night and a day were before her! What horror, what despair! For her father was all the world to her. He was all that she had. I could only pray that the exertions she was making, the fatigue that she was enduring, the pains of endless journeys would dull the shock when it came, and that she would not be able to feel or to suffer or to hate as at other times.

I believe that during these hours Paton kept guard outside, and warned off the curious. For no one came near us, and all the sounds of the camp seemed dull and distant and we two alone in the world, until a little before three o'clock. Then Tom returned. I had made a note that he must be kept at hand, since she would need him to go with her in my place when she knew all — as she must know all after she had seen her father.

I cautioned him as to this, but the man demurred.

"Marse, I'm feared ter do it," he said, showing the whites of his eyes in his earnestness. "Madam 'Stantia, she ordered me ter stay yer. En I'm tired, Marse. I'm en ole nigger en dis jurney's shuk me. Fer sho' it has."

"But you rogue, your mistress!"

"I 'bliged ter stay, Marse," he repeated doggedly. "Dis nigger's mighty tired."

I should have insisted, but the girl had heard his voice and summoned him. She opened her door and he went into the inner room. They talked there for some minutes, while I fretted over this new difficulty. Presently the black came out but she still remained within, and did not follow him for five long minutes. When she came I saw a change in her. Her eyes were bright, and each white cheek had its scarlet patch. She looked like a person in a fever, or on the edge of delirium. What the wine had not done, something else had effected.

"Tom had better be ready to ride with us," I said.

"No," she answered. "It will not be necessary. I wish him to stay here."

She spoke with so much decision that I could not contest the point, and we set off towards Wilmer's prison. All that I remember of our progress is that once we had to stand aside while a wing of the 23rd marched by; and that once we ran into a knot of blacks in front of the store. They were drunk and to my amazement refused to make way for us. My one arm did not avail much, but a couple of sergeants who were passing on the other side of the way crossed over and laying their canes about the rogues' shoulders, sent them flying down the road. I thanked the two, they saluted the lady, and we went on.

That is all that I remember of our seven or eight minutes walk. My mind was bent on the old question — what she would do when she learned my part in the matter. Would she take Tom — doubtless with a little delay we could find him? Or would she travel alone, riding the thirty-five miles, many of them after night-fall, unaccompanied? Or — or what would she do? Then, and all the long minutes during which she was with her father in the house opposite the tavern — where a sentry at the front and back declared the importance of the prisoner — I turned this question over and over and inside and out. Webster's quarters were at the tavern, a long low straggling building, set on a corner, with two fronts; and I might have entered and waited there. But nothing was farther from my mind. The thought of company, of the camp chatter, was abominable to me; and I paced up and down in a solitude which a glance at my face was enough to preserve.

THE WOMAN'S PART

She came out at last when my back was turned, and she reached my elbow unseen. "I am late," she said. "We should be on horseback by this time, Major Craven. Let us lose no time, if you please."

Surprised, I muttered assent, and I stole a look at her. Her eyes were bright, but with excitement not with tears. The patches of scarlet on her cheeks were more marked. I had expected to see her broken and pale with weeping; instead she was tense, borne up by the fever of some secret hope, more beautiful than I had ever seen her, more alive, more alert.

As for me I was now convinced that she knew all. Nay, enlightened at last, I saw that she must have known all from the start. Had she not foreseen that my coming boded ill? Had she not done all in her power to keep me at the Bluff? Had she not on that last evening strained all to detain me? Yes, she had known; and only my obtuseness, only the astonishing way in which she had placed herself in my hands and made use of me, had blinded me to the truth.

And plainly, she was content to go with me and to use me still. I might fancy if I chose, that she forgave me, but I did not dare to think so. There was a hardness in her eyes, a challenge in her voice, a reserve in her bearing as she walked beside me, silent and proud, that I misdoubted. And how could she forgive me? To her I was her father's murderer, a monster of ingratitude, a portent of falseness. She could not forgive. Enough that she did not flinch from me, that she was ready to bear with me, that she was willing to use me a little longer.

We found the horses standing before the door at Paton's quarters, and Tom with them. She bade the black farewell, after a few words aside with him, and ten minutes later we took the road on what I, for my part, knew to be a hopeless mission. Still it would serve, for it would help to pass these fatal hours; and afterwards she might comfort herself with the remembrance that she had done all in her power, that she had spent herself without stint or mercy in her father's service.

My latest impression of Winsboro', as I looked back before I settled myself in the saddle, was of Paton engaged in a last desperate argument with the Provost-Marshal. Only then did it occur to me that the unfortunate Marshal had had orders to place me under arrest and had been all day held at bay by my friend's good offices.

CHAPTER XI

THE MAN'S PART

The High Hills of Santee are a long irregular chain of Sand-hills on the left bank of the Wateree. Though directly above the noxious river the air on them is healthy and the water pure, making an oasis in the wide tract of miasma and fever in which the army had been operating.

LIFE OF GREENE.

It was not until we had left the camp a considerable distance behind us, and were clear of the neighboring roads with their stragglers and wagons and forage-parties that a word was spoken between us. Even that word turned only on the condition of the horses, the bay and grey that Paton had borrowed from the lines of the Fourteenth Dragoons. Let it be said of the British that, whatever their faults, they are magnanimous. The life of an enemy might depend — though I did not think, and hardly hoped that it would depend — on the speed of our horses. Yet the dragoons had lent us the best that they had, nor did I doubt that when the officer appeared on parade on the morrow, he would turn a blind eye on the gap in his ranks. It was I who broke the silence.

211

"They should carry us to the High Hills in six hours," I said.

The girl assented by a single word, uttered with an indifference which surprised me. And that was all.

Her silence had at least this advantage, that it left me free to consider her more closely, and I dropped back a horse's length that I might do this at my ease. As my eyes rested on her, I do not know whether my admiration or my wonder were the greater. She must have been weary to the bone and sick at heart. She must have been racked by suspense and torn by anxiety. Every nerve in her tender frame must have ached with pain, every pulse throbbed with fever. Probably, and almost certainly, she had had to face moments when hope failed her, and she saw things as they really were; when she tasted the bitterness of the coming hour and recognized that all her efforts to avert it were in vain.

Yet every line of her figure, the carriage of her head, the forward gaze of her eyes told but one tale of steadfast purpose. She was no longer a mere woman, subject to woman's weakness; but a daughter fighting for her father's life. She was love in action, moulded to its purest shape. To suffer the eye to dwell on the curling lock that stained the white of her neck, to give a thought to the long lashes that shaded her cheek, to eye the curve of her chin, or the slender fullness of her figure, seemed to be at this moment a sacrilege. Her sex had fallen from her, and she rode as safe in my company as if she had been a man. More, I reflected that if there were many like her on the rebel side — if there were others who, daughters of our race, grafted on its virtues the spirit of this new land, then, I had no doubt of the issue of the unhappy contest in which we were engaged. In that case the thirteen colonies were as safe from us and as certainly lost to His Majesty as if they were the six planets and the seven Pleiades.

Nor in anything, I reflected, was her firmness more plain than in her treatment of me. She knew what I had done. She knew that she owed her misery to me. She must hate me in her heart. And doubtless when she had used me she would cast me aside. But in the meantime and because my help was needful to her plans, she was content to use me. She was willing to speak to me, to ride beside me, to breathe the same air with me, she could bear the sound of my voice and the touch of my hand. She could constrain herself to stoop even to this, if by any means she might save the father she loved and whom I had betrayed!

But while she did this, she was as cold as a stone,

she made no pretence of friendship or of amity; and the light was failing, we had ridden ten miles, passing now a picket-guard, and now a lonely vedette on a hill-top, and many a sutler's cart on the road, before she spoke again. Then as we descended a gorge, following the winding of a mountain stream that brawled below us amid mosses and alders, and under fern-clad banks, she asked me if we should reach the ferry on the Wateree by eight.

She spoke to me over her shoulder, for she was riding a pace in front of me and I had made no effort to place myself on a level with her. "I am afraid not," I said. "If we reach the ferry by nine we shall be fortunate. Very soon it will be dark and we must go more slowly."

"Then let us push on while we can," she replied. And starting her horse with the spur she cantered down the uneven winding track, flinging the dirt and stones behind her, as if she had no neck and I had two arms. If she gave a thought to my drawback she must have decided that it was no time to consider it; as from her point of view it was not. Fortunately the sky was still pale and clear, the light had not quite failed, and presently without mishap we reached more level ground. Here the road, parting from the stream, wound on a level round the flank of a low hill, and for a mile or two we made fair progress. It was only when the darkness closed in on us at last that we drew rein, and trusting our horses' instincts rather than our own eyes pushed forward, now at a trot and now at a walk.

"When does the moon rise?" she asked presently.

"At eight," I told her.

"The ferry boat runs all night?"

Now I had not thought of that. It was a much-used ferry situate at a point where the traffic from Charlestown separated, a part of the traffic using the boat and crossing to the higher and drier road on the right bank, the rest pursuing the shorter but heavier way through Camden. As a second route the ferry road was of value, and a considerable portion of our supplies came in that way. I knew that there was a half company of the 33rd posted to protect the crossing, but I remembered that the ferry house was on the farther or eastern bank. Probably the detachment also would be on that side.

I had to tell her this, and that I was not sure that the ferry ran at night. "I hope," I added, "that we shall be able to make the men hear, if it does not. But if we fail we may be detained."

"All night?" she asked and I thought that I read in her tone not only anxiety but contempt — contempt of my ignorance and inefficiency. "Do you mean that?"

I told her that I feared that we might be detained until day-break; and with pity I wondered how, fatigued as she was, she would be able to endure a night in the open. "Still, it is not more than two leagues," I continued, " from the river to the hills, and when we are across the stream we should travel the remainder of the distance in an hour."

Her only answer was a weary sigh. A minute later we passed from the darkness of the night, which has always a certain transparency, into the black depths of a pinewood. In an instant it was impossible to see a yard before us. The carpet of leaves deadened the sound of the horses' hoofs, the air was close, and great moths flew into our faces. I pictured bats, the large bats of Carolina, swinging past our heads. The whip-poor-will warned us again and again from the depth of the forest. Still for a time the horses stepped on daintily, feeling their way and snorting at intervals. At last the grey stopped. It refused to proceed. "We must lead the horses," I said.

"I will," she cried quickly. "You have only one arm." And before I could remonstrate I heard her slip from her saddle.

So she had not after all forgotten my arm.

But it was humiliating, it was depressing to follow while she led. And the way seemed to be end-

216

less. Once I heard her stumble. She uttered a low cry and the grey shied away from her. She mastered it again, and anew she went forward, though with each moment I expected her to propose that we should halt until the moon rose. Still she persisted, bent on her purpose, and after a long stage of this strange traveling we came forth into the light again. She climbed into the saddle. The horses flung up their heads as they scented the freshness and perfume of the night, and we broke into a trot. I rode up beside her. It was then or a little later, when we had slackened our speed on rising ground that she began to talk to me.

Not freely, but with constraint and an under-note of bitterness which her story explained. At dawn on the morning after my departure from the Bluff she had started to ride to Winnsboro' to warn her father of his danger. Unfortunately, when she and Tom had traveled a dozen miles they had fallen in with a band of straggling Tories — one of Brown's bands from Ninety-six, she believed. These men, knowing her to be Wilmer's daughter and having a grudge against him — and doing no worse than the other side did — had forced her and Tom to dismount and had taken their horses, telling them that they were lucky to escape with no other ill-treatment.

Thus stranded on the way, the two had walked seven miles to a friendly plantation, only to learn that there, too, the horses had been swept off by the same gang of Tories. In the end they had been forced to return to the Bluff on foot. Here there were horses indeed, but they were out on the hill and perforce she rested while they were found and brought in. Again the pair set out, but twenty-four hours had been lost, and ten miles short of the camp she learned from friends that she was too late. A man whom she had no difficulty in conjecturing to be her father had been seized, tried and sentenced on the previous day.

It was a pitiful story of effort, of strain, of failure, and she told it piece-meal, with long intervals of silence as her feelings or the condition of the road dictated. In the telling we covered a good part of the journey, now riding freely over hills clothed with low brushwood, where myrtles and dogwood and sweet herbs, crushed by the passage of our horses, filled the air with fragrance, now plodding through the gloom of oak-woods where the notes of the mocking-bird brought the English nightingale to mind; and now — this more often at the last — crossing patches of low country where masses of tall cypress, black in the moonlight, betrayed the presence of swamps, and where the voices of a thousand frogs, challenging, insistent, unceasing, bade us look to our going. We were descending quickly from the uplands to the low country of South Carolina, the home of the rice-fields and of fever; and except the High Hills of Santee, scarcely a rising ground of any size now stood between us and Charles Town neck, ninety odd miles distant.

If she could not tell her tale without agitation I could not hear it without pain, and pain that grew the keener, as I saw that in the telling she was working herself into a fiercer mood. Once or twice a bitter word fell from her and betrayed the soreness she felt; and these complaints, I came to think, were uttered with intention. If I had soothed myself at any time with the thought that she did not see events as I saw them, if I had tried to believe that she accepted my help willingly, I was now convinced that I might dismiss the notion. It was no fancy of mine that she shrank from me.

It was at the moment when she had let fall the most cruel of these gibes, that she pulled up the gray and changed the subject, asking me abruptly if we had lately passed a road on the left.

I told her — I could not answer her with spirit — that I had not observed one.

"What time is it?" was her next question.

It was nearly nine, I answered.

"We pass through a village before we reach the ferry, do we not?" she asked.

"There should be a house or two about a mile before us," I explained.

After that she rode on in silence. But when we had traveled another half mile we came to a post set up at a corner; and there a by-way on the left did run into our road. By this time the moon was high and the sign-post stood up white and ghastly. "Here is the turning," she said, reining in her horse. "Do you know this road?"

"Only that it is not ours," I answered wondering what she had in her mind.

"I am not sure of that," she replied abruptly. "There is an old ferry half a mile up the stream, and I am told that this road leads to it. Ten years ago the present ferry crossed there, but it was moved to a point lower down to shorten the road. Now do you see?"

"What?" I asked.

"That we might cross the river there. The boat is on this side, I believe. Whereas if we go to the new ferry and can make no one hear, we shall be detained until morning."

I was considerably taken aback both by her knowledge of the district and by a proposal so unlooked for. Moreover, I had never heard of a second ferry, though there might be one. "I think if we are wise we shall keep to the high road," I said prudently, "and go to the proper ferry. At any rate we ought to go as far as the hamlet. We can learn there if the ferry be working, and if it is not we may be able to secure a boat. We don't know the old crossing — "

"Are you afraid?" she asked.

The taunt did not affect me. "No," I said, "but a ferry at night, if it is seldom worked, and the man is old too, — well, it is not the safest of ventures."

"A ferry in good moonlight!" she cried in scorn. "Are you afraid, sir? When the risk is mine and if I do not reach the High Hills in time it will not be you who will pay the penalty?"

I could not meet that argument, nor the passion in her voice. Yet I remember that I hesitated. The place was forbidding. We were halfway down the slope that led to the river, and below us stretched the marshes that fringed the stream, marshes always dreary and deceitful, and at night veiled in poisonous mists. At the foot of the sign-post, which rose pale and stark against a background of pines, there was something which had the look of a newly-dug grave; while halfway up the mast a wisp of stuff, the relic, perhaps, of a flag which had been nailed up and torn down, fluttered dismally in the wind. I looked along the main road but no one was stirring. The lights of the hamlet were not in sight.

I suspected that, quietly as she sat her horse, she was in suspense until I answered, and I gave way. "Very well," I said reluctantly. "But you must not blame me if we go wrong. God knows I only want to do the best for you?"

I do not know why my words displeased her, but they seemed to prick her in some tender spot.

"The best?" she cried, "and you boast of that? You!"

"God forbid," I said, breaking in on her speech. "If there were more I could do, I would do it and gladly, but —"

"Don't! Don't!" she said, pain in her tone. And she turned her horse's head and plodded down the side-road in silence. I followed.

Still I was uneasy. The night, the loneliness, the scene, all chilled me; and this tardy suggestion, this change of plan at the last moment had an odd look. However I reflected that I had nothing to lose; the loss was hers if we were not in time. And though a one-armed man in an old and rotten ferry-boat — so I pictured the craft we were to enter — is not very happily placed, if she did not see this, I could not raise the point.

222

My perplexity grew, however, when twenty minutes' riding failed to bring us to the river, though the
road had by this time sunk to the marshes, and ran
deep and foundrous, lapped on either side by sullen
pools. The time came when I drew rein — I would
go no farther; the air was laden with ague, I felt it
in my bones. "I don't think we are right," I said.

"You would do so much!" she cried bitterly.
"But you won't do this for me."

"I will do anything that will be of service, Miss
Wilmer," I said firmly, "but to waste our time here
will not be of serivce."

"What will?" she wailed. "Will anything?"
Then, stopping me as I was about to answer, "There!
a light!" she cried. "Do you see? There is a
light before us! We can inquire."

She was right, there was a light. Nay, when we
had advanced a few yards we saw that there were
two lights, which proceeded from the windows of
some building. I was grateful for the discovery,
grateful for anything that put an end to the contest between us; and "Thank God!" I said as
cheerfully as I could. "Now we shall learn where
we are, and we can decide what to do."

"More, there is the river," she added; and a
moment later I, too, caught the gleam of moonlight
on a wide water, that flowed on the farther side, as

it seemed to me, of the spot whence the lights issued.

I was glad to see it, and I said so. I could discern the building now — a gaunt, dark block set high against the sky; a mill apparently, for a skeleton frame of ribs rose against one end of it. The lights that we had seen issued irom two windows at some distance from the ground and not far apart. As well as I could judge, the building stood between road and river on piles, with a rood or so of made ground to landward, and a few wind-bent cypresses fringing the river bank behind. It was a lonely house, and dark and forbidding by night; but by day it might be cheerful enough.

"I will inquire," I said, briskly slipping from my saddle. "You had better wait here, while I go," I added.

I was in the act of leading my horse towards the door, when she thrust out her hand and seized my rein. "Stop!" she said. And then for a moment she did not speak.

I obeyed; for the one word she had uttered conveyed to me, I don't know how, that a new peril threatened us. "Why?" I muttered. "What is it?" I looked about us. I could see nothing alarming. I turned to her.

She sat low in the saddle, her head sunk on her

breast, and for a moment I fancied that she was ill. Then in a low, despairing tone, "I cannot," she muttered, speaking rather to herself than to me, "I cannot do it."

I stared at her. To fail now, to succumb now — she who had borne up so well, gone through so much, endured so bravely! "I am afraid I do not understand," I said. "What is the matter, Miss Wilmer?"

Her head sank lower. By such light as there was I could see that the spirit had gone out of her, that her courage had left her, and hope. "I cannot do it," she said again. "God forgive me!"

"What? What cannot you do!" I asked, carried away by my impatience.

"Let us go back," she said. "We will go back." And she began to turn her horse's head.

But that was absurd, and out of the question, now that we were here; and in my turn I caught her rein. Here was the ferry, here were persons who could direct us. Had we traveled so far, and were we at the last moment, because a house looked dark and lonely, to lose heart and retrace our steps? "Go back?" I said. "Surely not without some reason, Miss Wilmer? Surely not without knowing —"

"Without knowing what?" she replied, cutting

225

me short. "Why we are here?" And then in a different tone, "Do you know, sir, why we are here?"

"No," I said, in astonishment. For she who had all day been so calm, so cool, so steadfast, now spoke with a wildness that alarmed me. "Why?"

"To put you," she replied, "into the power of those with whom you will fare as my father fares! Do you understand, sir? To make you a hostage for him, your life for his life, your freedom for his freedom! Do you know that there are those, in yonder house, who are waiting for you, — who are waiting for you, and who, if my father suffers, will do to you as your friends do to him? Do you know that it was for that that I brought you hither; yes, for that! And now, now that I am here, I cannot do it —" her voice sank to a whisper — "even to save my father!"

A dry painful sob shook her in the saddle. She clung to the pommel, the reins fell from her hands, the tired horse under her hung its head. "Good Lord!" I whispered. "Good Lord! And you brought me here for that."

"Yes," she said, "for that."

"And — and Lord Cornwallis — you knew that you had nothing to expect from him?" She bowed her head. "But did you not know, Miss Wilmer, that this — this, too, was hopeless? Insane, mad? Did you not know that Lord Rawdon would as soon depart from his duty in order to save me, as the sun from his course?"

"Men have been saved that way," she cried, with something of her old spirit. "And you are his friend, sir, you have influence, you have rank, oh, he would do much to save you! Yes, I might have saved my father! I might have preserved him — and now!" her chin sank again upon her breast.

"It was a mad plot!" I said.

"But it might have saved him," she whispered. "My lord spoke warmly of you, he shewed me your sword on the table. Yes, I might have saved my father — but I could not do it. And now —" Her voice died away.

"It was a mad plot," I repeated. However strong her belief, I, of course, knew that such a step was hopeless; that no danger in which I might stand would turn Rawdon from his duty, but on the contrary would stiffen him in it. It was a mad plan. But apparently she had believed in it, apparently she had trusted in it; and at the last she had been unable to harden her heart to carry it through! Why? I asked myself the question.

She sighed, and the sound went to my heart. She gathered up her reins. "We had better go,

227

sir," she said, in a lifeless tone, "before they discover our presence. They may hear our voices."

She had not had the strength to carry it through!
Why? My heart beat more quickly as I pondered
the question. I no longer felt the fog on my cheek,
the ague in my bones. The note of the bull-frog
lost its melancholy, the sigh of the wind across the
marshes its sadness. Warmth awoke in me, and
with it hope, and a purpose — a purpose, wild it
might be, high-strained it might be, and extravagant, but deliberate. For as certainly as I loved her,
as certainly as my heart-strings were torn for the
tenderness of her body broken by so many fatigues,
for the agony of her spirit which had borne her so
far, as certainly as she was heaven and earth to me
— and she loved me, I believed it now! — so surely
did I know that there was but one bridge which
could cross the gulf that divided me from her!
There was one way, and one way only, which could
bring me to her.

And that way lay through the door of the mill.
Yet first — first, strong as my purpose was, I had to
fight the temptation to pay myself a part of that
which fate might withhold from me. To clasp her
knees as I stood beside her, to draw her down to me,
to hold her on my breast, to cover her face, white
and woe-begone in the moonlight, with kisses, to tell

her that I loved her — this had been heaven to me!
But I had to forego it. I might not pay myself
beforehand. Afterwards — but I dared not think
of afterwards. I dared not think of what lay between the present and the future. I must act, not
think.

"We had better go," she repeated dully.

"And you thought it might save him?" I said.

"I thought that I could do it!" she answered.
She shivered.

"You shall do it," I replied. "Come!"

I led my horse towards the door, and had travelled half the space that lay between us and the
threshold before she grasped my meaning; before
she moved. Then, "Stop!" she cried. She pressed
her horse abreast of me. "Don't you understand?" she cried. "Don't you see —"

"Yes," I said, "I see." And for a moment, as we
passed from the moonlight into the shadow, and the
horses' shoes clattered on the stones before the door,
I let my hand rest on her knee. "I see. But I also
remember. I remember that your father saved my
life. I remember that I delivered him up to death.
I remember — many things. And if any risk of
mine may avail to save him, God knows that I take
the hazard cheerfully!"

She cried, "No!" with a sort of passion, and

she tried to draw me back. But it was too late. I was at the door. I kicked it.

"House!" I cried. "House!" My mind was made up. Whatever came of it, whatever the issue, I would go through with the venture.

Immediately a light shone under the door, a voice cried, "Halloa!" And while, stammering words half-heard, the girl still tried to turn me from my purpose, the door was opened, and a light was flashed in my face. A man confronted me on the threshold, two others slipped by me into the darkness. Probably the purpose of the latter was to cut off my retreat, but I paid no heed to them.

"Can you direct us to the ferry?" I said.

"Why not?" the man drawled. "Step inside, sir. Ben will hold your horse. And a lady? Well, we did not expect to see company and we'll do the best we can. We shall not be for letting you go in a hurry," he added with meaning in his tone.

It was not my cue to notice the sneer, or to show suspicion, and I followed the man into the lower room of the mill, a damp stable-like place, where the light fell on the shining, startled eyes of a row of horses tethered at a rack. I ran my eye along them; it was well to know what force I had against me. There were six. We passed behind their heels, and picking our way over the filthy floor followed the man up a ladder to what appeared to be the living-room of the place. As I climbed I heard above me a sharp question and an exultant answer; and, I confess, my heart sank, for I recognized the voice that put the question. It was with no surprise, and certainly it was with no pleasure, that emerging from the trap I found myself face to face with my old acquaintance, Levi.

There were two more of the gang with him — I knew them again. The three men were seated on boxes before a fire, the smoke from which found a leisurely exit through a broken chimney of clay. The walls were formed of squared logs, the shingled roof was festooned with cobwebs. In one corner lay a heap of dirty cornstraw, in another a pile of driftwood. The floor was a litter of broken casks and cases, with some rotting gear and fishing-nets, and a keg or two.

Levi made me a mock bow. "Evening, Major," he said, "Well, well, you surely never know your luck! Never know when you're going to meet old friends! I'm d — d if we'll part this time as easily as we did last time!"

"We only want the ferry," I said, playing out my part.

"Oh!" he cried rudely. "Our duty to you, and hang the ferry! We've wanted you mightily, Major, and now you are here we mean to keep you. Here, sirree, get up," he continued, kicking the box from under one of the other men, "Let the lady sit down. Cannot you see that she's dog-weary?"

The man moved awkwardly out of the way.

"The Captain will have a high opinion of you, Ma'am," Levi continued in an oily tone that made me long to wring his neck. "If you'll be bidden by me, you will allow me to offer you a sup of Kentucky whisky. It's the queen of liquors to bring the color back to your cheeks."

She did not decline the offer; no doubt she needed support. He put a cloak on the box and she sat down with her back to me, either to play her part the better, or because she could not bear to face me. None the less could I picture the ordeal through which she was passing! Levi, fussing about her, brought out a bottle and drawing the corn-cob cork poured some of the spirit into a small bowl. She drank it and said something to him in a low voice.

"Pete is saddling his horse now," he answered. "He's a mighty good man in the saddle, and he'll not spare his spurs. He'll take the message! But we shall need a piece of the fur to prove that the bear is trapped. Here you," he went on truculently, turning to me, "You are in our power and we are going to hold you as a hostage for Wilmer.

Do you understand? If your folks hang him, we shall hang you! Do you see? Have I spoken plainly, sir?"

"Plainly enough," I said. "But you must be very foolish if you think that that will do Captain Wilmer any good; if you think that a threat of that kind will make Lord Rawdon hold his hand."

"D—n my lord and his hand!" he retorted coarsely; and he spat on the floor. "My lord will decide as he pleases. But as he decides, you, Major, will hang or go free. So, by your leave do you write and tell your folks what I say."

"If I write," I replied, "I shall tell his lordship to do his duty."

"Major," he answered. "Do you see that fire? We have means to persuade you and if you try us too far —"

"I shall not write," I said. "If I write those are my terms. That is what I shall write. But if it's only proof that I am in your hands that you require, take my ring. It will be known and will do what you want. Only I warn you, my friend, that the man who carries the message will slip his neck into a noose."

"Do you think that we don't know that!" Levi replied, grinning. "We need no Philadelphia lawyer to teach us our business. This country is ours—ours,

Englishman, and it is going to remain ours. We have ten friends where King George has one, and we shall know how to place your ring where we want it. Many is the time that I've laughed to think of Wilmer fighting your quails for you, and you putting on the money, and your bird not worth a continental cent!"

The girl raised her head. She said something that I could not hear.

"To be sure, Miss," he answered obsequiously. "To be sure, time is running. Here, give me the ring." He weighed it a minute in his hand and his eyes sparkled as if he had no mind to part with it. Then he turned to the ladder. The girl rose too. "I will speak to Pete," she said.

"We need not trouble you," he answered. "You sit down, Ma'am, and rest."

"I will speak to Pete," she said again, as if he had not spoken. And carefully averting her face from me — I wondered if she knew how deeply, how pitifully I felt for her — she followed Levi down the ladder.

CHAPTER XII

THE MILL ON THE WATEREE

With what a leaden and retarding weight
Does expectation load the wing of Time.

MASON.

The thing was done, for good or ill; it remained for me to make the best of it. I was in Levi's power, but I might still by firmness hold my own for a time. Thinking of this, I turned a case on end, dusted it cooly with the skirt of my coat and setting it near the fire, I sat down on it and warmed myself. The men who had been left with me watched me curiously but did not interfere. They were busy, cooking something in a pot by the light of a wick burning in a bowl of green wax. Meantime, the minutes passed slowly; very slowly, while I waited and listened for news of the others. Five, ten, fifteen minutes went by before the clatter of horses' shoes on the stones of the paved yard told us that Pete had started. A little later Constantia climbed the ladder, and appeared, closely followed by Levi, and by another man who was doubtless one of those who had slipped by me at the door.

The girl paused on reaching the floor, then deliberately she came forward and chose a seat on the opposite side of the fire and as far from mine as possible. Levi grinned. "Well, Major," he said "Pete's gone, whip and spur! If you've sense enough you'll wish him luck."

"I do," I said cooly, "but as that matter is not very pressing, and I am hungry, uncommonly hungry —"

"It'll be mighty pressing this time to-morrow," he grinned. "You've twenty-four hours, and may make the most of it! Then, if things don't go our way!"

"I understand," I said. "But in the meantime, my man, I am more interested in my supper. The lady, too, has been riding for six hours —"

"Oh, the lady?" he sneered. "You bear no malice it seems?"

"At any rate I will keep it until I am free," I answered, carefully averting my eyes from her.

"If that time comes?" he retorted.

"Just so," I said.

I think it was his purpose to make me angry; but at this point one of the others, the ruffian who had kept watch in the outer room on the night of the outrage at the Bluff, struck in. "Make an end!" he growled with an oath. "Isn't it enough," addressing me, "that you've the use of your throat to-night that you must argy, argy, argy! Keep your breath to cool your victuals, stranger — while you have it! And, curse me, you're as bad, Levi! Let's have an end! And do you," to the men at the fire, "get on with that pork and hominy!"

The girl did not say a word. She sat somewhat apart wrapped in a cloak and leaning forward. Her elbow rested on her knee, her chin on her hand, her eyes were fixed on the fire. The pose was one of utter weariness and dejection, but it was so natural, so unforced that she might have been sitting in the room alone. She seemed to be unconscious not only of my presence but of the presence of the men. And they, rough and desperate as they were, stood evidently in awe of her. As they moved to and fro about their cooking they passed close to her, and at times they swore. But I could see that their ease was assumed. Her personality, her tragic position, the respect in which women are held in the southern colonies, were as a wall about her — for the present.

And what was she thinking, I wondered, as she sat, apparently as heedless of me, as of the men who rubbed elbows with her? Was she thinking only of her father and his peril, and of the chance which her passing weakness had come so near to forfeiting? Was she weighing that chance between hope and fear, and with no thought except of him who lay in the prison house opposite the tavern at Winnsboro'? Or was she dreaming of me as well as of her father? Thinking of me with pity, with gratitude, with — love? Had I built the bridge? Had I crossed the gulf?

I could not say, seeing her so still, so remote, so passionless. At any rate I could not be sure. The whole width of the hearth divided us, and she sat with her face turned from me. Not a glance of her veiled eyes sped my way, and apparently she was not conscious of my presence. So that by and by that of which I had been confident a little earlier began to seem doubtful, a dream, a mere delusion on my part.

And yet it might be true! It might be that I did exist for her, largely, filling the room, shutting out her view of the men about us, encroaching even on her sense of her father's peril. It might be so. At any rate it was to this question that my whole mind was directed — what was she thinking of me? What were the thoughts behind that averted face? Was I still the betrayer of her father? Or — or what was I?

Presently the men began to pour the mess which they had cooked into rough bowls, and for a time the steam, savoury enough to the senses of a hungry man, switched off my thoughts. I took note of the room, while I awaited my turn. The smoke of the drift-wood fire, mingling with the fog that eddied in from the marshes, hid the roof, but the air below was tolerably clear. The men had propped their guns against the wall opposite me and I counted them. There were five. An active man, I thought, might have cast himself between the arms and their owners, and snatching a gun might have held off the five — Levi, I knew, was a white-livered cur. But a crippled man could not do this; nor, as I found a moment later when one of the men thrust a bowl and a hunch of corn-bread on my lap, could he with any success cut up tough pork with a pocket-knife.

The cooking was coarse, but I was famished, and I wrestled manfully with the difficulty. I did so to little purpose, however. The bowl slipped on my knees, I could not steady it. A man sniggered, another laughed. They stopped eating to look at me. At that I lost patience. "Will you cut it for me?" I said, holding out the bowl to the nearest man.

He refused — the truth was my difficulty entertained their clownish souls. "D — n me, cut your own victuals," he answered churlishly. "Enough, that I've cooked 'em for you."

239

"Be thankful you've a throat to swallow 'em with!" said a second.

The others laughed; and at that, I who had taken with coolness their threat to murder me, felt such a rage rise within me, helpless as I was, that the tears stood in my eyes. I looked at Constantia.

There was the faintest stain of color in her cheeks, but apparently she was unconscious of what was passing. Still and self-contained, she was eating and drinking with the steady purpose of one who was set on maintaining her strength. As quickly as anger had risen, it died in me, and, alas, my heart sank with it. The men might jeer and taunt and laugh, I no longer cared. I finished my meal as I could, heeding their amusement as little as she did. For the savor had left the food. I saw that I must have been mistaken. Yes, I must have been mistaken. She could not care for me.

When all was eaten Levi went down with two of the men to set a guard, and he was absent for some time. When he returned, wood was put on the fire and the lamp was extinguished. For a time he and the men remained apart talking in low voices, but soon, one by one, they left the group, pulled cloaks or blankets about them and lay down — one of them across the trap-door. Levi made the girl some offer of accommodation, but she refused it, and dragging a second box to the fire, to eke out the first, she made a rough couch, on which she sat with her feet raised and her back against the wall. I lay on the opposite side of the fire, some way from her; and at times I fancied that her eyes dwelt on me. But I could not be sure, for her face, half shrouded by her cloak and in shadow, was hard to distinguish; while I, when I looked that way, met the light.

If I had been sure that her eyes were upon me, if I had been sure that she thought of me and thanked me, I could have faced the prospect more lightly. But I had no certainty of this; I had, indeed, much reason to doubt it, and I looked forward to a night of suspense. I foresaw that as the warmth died in me and the small hours chilled my bones and damped my resolution, I should repent of what I had done. A man snored, another muttered in his sleep, the mosquitoes troubled me. At intervals a horse moved restlessly in the stable below. A marsh-owl, hunting along the river bank, tore the night from time to time with its shrill screech. I had no hope of sleep.

The danger that is thrust on a man, he must meet. But the danger into which, being no hero, he has thrust himself, is another matter. I knew that long before morning, I should feel that I had cast away my life. Thoughts of Osgodby and England, visions of home faces, now thousands of miles

241

away, would rise to reproach me. I should see —
with that terrible four o'clock in the morning clear-
ness — that for a fancy, for a woman's whim, for a
fantastic point of honor, I had done what I had no
right to do; I had sacrificed my life and all that I
had valued a short time back. I should remember
that she had scarcely touched my hand in friendship,
had never listened to a word of love, never said even
that she forgave me!

But blessed be the soldier's habit of making the
best of the present! In half an hour, before the
strangeness of the situation had quite worn off,
before her near neighborhood, at another time so
disturbing, had grown familiar, before the owl's
sharp note had ceased to startle, I dozed. And
presently worn out by strain — for sorrow sleeps
soundly — I fell into a deep slumber which lasted
until long after daylight.

When I awoke there were only two men in the
room. They were chopping up drift-wood in a
corner, and it was the sound of their hatchets that
had roused me. The fire had burned low on the
hearth, and my teeth chattered. A fog filled the
outer world, poured in through the windows, laid
a clammy touch on everything. Firelight had done
much the night before to redeem the squalor of the
room; this morning, daylight showed it in all its

cold and grisly reality. And where was Constantia? Where was Levi? I crossed the room to one of the windows and I looked out. They might be below. But at a distance of five yards the eye plunged into a sea of mist. I could see nothing, and I turned about, shivering, the cold in my bones.

"You're a mighty good sleeper," one of the men said as I met his eye.

"I was tired."

"Well, it would be more than I could manage!" he answered cryptically. "Do you think they'll let him go!"

"Captain Wilmer?"

He nodded. He was a shock-headed man in a frayed hunting shirt, buckskin leggings and mocassins. A greasy ragged unshaven figure of a man.

"No," I said, "I'm sure they will not. Would you?"

"D—d if I would," he answered, grinning. "I never let a 'possum go yet that I got a grip of! But you've spunk, I'll say that!"

The other man turned and silenced him with an oath, but I marked the speaker for the best-natured of the band. Something might be made of him, at a pinch. Meanwhile the two, having finished their task, stirred up the embers, piled on wood and started the fire. When they had done this I crouched miserably enough over the blaze, while the two went about getting a meal. I noticed that the guns had been removed. It struck me that, were I only fifty yards away in this fog I should be safe from pursuit. But how was I to win those fifty yards!

As I thought of this and with my mind's eye measured the height from the windows to the ground, I heard voices below, and after a short interval Constantia came up the ladder, muffled in her cloak. She did not look in my direction, but she came straight to the fire and stooped over it to warm her hands. Then, hardly moving her lips, and choosing a moment when the two men had turned their backs, "Be close to me," she breathed "if trouble comes. Keep away now."

She moved some paces from me as soon as she had spoken, and when Levi and the other two men appeared, we were standing on opposite sides of the hearth. Levi cast a sharp glance at me; I think he had his suspicions — God knows what had roused them when I had seen nothing! But he only swore at the men for letting down the fire and at the fire for giving no warmth, and at the morning for being cold. If ever there was an ill-conditioned cur, he was one!

For me, I was no longer cold. Her words, her tone, tingled through my veins, set my pulses beating, did all but give strength to my useless arm. I could face anything now, I could face the worst now, and hope to live through it.

My relief, indeed, was unspeakable. But apart from me — and I masked my feelings — it was a gloomy party that, shivering in the aguish air, gathered about the poor meal and ate and drank in a brutish fashion. Constantia kept her old place on the farther side of the hearth, and muffled in her cloak preserved a stern silence. Her face by the morning light looked white and drawn, so that even in a lover's eyes it lacked something of its ordinary beauty. But the strain which she was putting on herself did not appear until the meal was over, and we had risen from our seats. Then when the men, stuffing their corn-cob pipes, had gone, some to feed the horses, and some to lean yawning from the windows and curse the fog, she began to walk up and down the room; while Levi watched her openly and I in secret. To and fro, she paced, the hood of her cloak drawn over her head, to and fro, this way and that, restlessly; only breaking her march at intervals to glance from the window and sigh, and so to resume her walk.

"There'll be no news yet, ma'am," Levi said after a time. He spoke with servility but I guessed that he was suspicious and uneasy. I wondered if he had intercepted some glance meant for me.

She gave him no answer by word or look. She continued to walk up and down. Impatience seemed to be getting the better of her. She could not be still.

"They'll be having the message, about this time," he said, glancing at me in turn. "Not a minute earlier."

I nodded. I had no doubt that he was right.

"Curse me," he continued, "but as sure as there are snakes in Virginia, you're a cool fish, Major! You mightn't have a tongue in your head. What is it, I'd like to know, you have up your sleeve?"

I laughed. It was easy to laugh since she had spoken to me.

The man with the buckskin shirt was sitting on the sill of the farther window, swinging his feet. He began to whistle. The girl stopped in her walk, as if she had been struck. She looked at him with something in her face that was equal to a man's worst oath. Then, "oh, hush!" she said. "Hush!"

The fellow stared at her in astonishment, but he ceased to whistle. She stood. For a minute or two there was no sound in the room except the bubbling of a foul pipe, no sound outside but the wailing cry of a waterfowl. It was the mallard's cry that she had heard, perhaps; for presently she resumed her walk, Levi still watching her with a crafty eye. If she was listening he was thinking, and it was then for the first time that it struck me with something of a shock that he was not the man to let me go — however Wilmer might fare. A bad thought that, to intrude at this time!

One of the horses pawed restlessly in the room below, and the man who had gone down to feed them, shouted a question from the foot of the ladder. Levi answered him. The interruption this caused brought the same look of impatience, of endurance, of sheer suffering to the girl's face. She stood, she turned to me; for the first time, as if she could no longer control herself, she spoke to me openly. "What time is it?" she asked.

"Half past ten," I said. "I fear that you cannot expect news yet." I was moved indeed, moved to the heart with pity for her; and pained, in the midst of my own anxiety, to think that she should pass intolerable hours in expecting what could not come yet — and in my view would not come at all. By and by things would be better. The sun would suck up the vapors, we should breathe more freely, we should be able to look abroad, we should see something if it were but the sun-lit marshes. As it was, the grizly room, the choking fog, the men, the suspense, set the worst face on everything and filled me with loathing.

Presently a flight of birds passed the house with a whirring of wings and a single note of alarm. The man at the window leant out to follow them with his eye. He muttered something about a gun, and again there was silence, while Constantia resumed her restless march, and Levi followed her with his eyes.

A long, long quarter of an hour followed, and then the silence was broken. Out of the fog came a faint whooping cry, distant and tremulous. The girl was the first to hear it and she stood, as if turned to stone. I saw her stiffen, I saw her eyes dilate, her lips grow white. Her gaze met mine in an agony of questioning. For a moment she ceased to breathe, so intently she listened. Then the cry rose again, still distant but louder. She turned to the trap-door, as if to go down.

But her limbs failed her — at any rate Levi was before her. I suppose he had studied her as closely as I had. He bounded to the head of the ladder, and slipped down it, calling out to her that he would see what it was, calling out to the remaining man to look to me. The girl, thus forestalled, turned from the ladder, and went to the window. She leant on the sill, and I saw that she was shaking from head to foot. "It is Tom!" she murmured.

"Tom!" I exclaimed.

"Yes! Tom!" she said, her breath coming in sobs. "He has news. Oh, God in His mercy grant that it be good news!"

We saw Levi and two of the men run from the house, and vanish in the fog that hid the road. We heard the cry once more — it was near at hand now — but there followed on it a confused outcry, a thudding of feet, a shot — the flame of which for an instant rent the mist — a struggle. The girl sank against me, and if I had not put my arm round her and supported her, she would have fallen. "It was Tom!" she gasped. "It was Tom!"

"Then there's some foul play on foot!" I cried.

"Yes, foul play," she whispered. "They'll not let us have the news! They'll keep the news from us!" For a moment I thought that she would collapse altogether, but as suddenly as she had given way, she recovered. She drew a deep fluttering breath, released herself from my arm, stood up. She glanced, pale and frowning, at the man who leant from the other window. He, too, was striving to make out what was passing, and from time to time he gave vent to his excitement in an oath. He had forgotten us, and forgotten his duty, too, if it was to guard us. While one might count five she considered him; then deftly, with her eyes still fixed on him she drew a pistol from some hidden

249

place in her dress, and slipped it into my hand. "Can you use it?" she whispered.

"Yes," I muttered.

Then, "Now!" she said.

I cocked it, saw that the priming was in its place, and took two steps towards the man. "Halloa!" I cried.

He drew in his head and found himself covered by the pistol; a pistol is a thing a one-armed man can use. "Go down!" I said. "Quick!" He opened his mouth to speak. "Quick, my man, go down!" I repeated. "Or — that's better!" I said, as, still covered by the muzzle he moved unwillingly to the head of the ladder, and began, swearing furiously, to descend. "Tell your rogue of a leader," I went on, "to come under the window and speak to me!"

I should have followed the man down, seen him out, and barred the outer door, thus securing the horses; but one of the gang was in the lower doorway, and though his attention was fixed on the scene that was passing outside I feared to lose all by trying to gain too much. Instead I waited until our man's head was below the level of the floor, then I dropped the pistol and shut down the trap upon him. As quickly as I did it, Constantia was at my elbow with the heaviest case she could drag forward. We set it on the trap-door, furiously piled a second on the top of it and a third on that. Then we looked at one another. Her eyes were gloomy. "They have killed him!" she exclaimed. "They have killed Tom!"

"I hope not," I said. "They may have fired to frighten him!"

"And the news!" she panted. She clasped her hands. "He brought news!"

The news? Ay, it was that which had done it! She was hungering, thirsting, parched for the news, and they kept it from her! She could have killed the men, for that! And yet, what news, I wondered, had she in her mind? What news could she expect at this hour of the day, when Pete could barely have delivered his message?

Still that was a small question beside the fact that I was out of the snare, was free, was armed. And she was with me, one with me, leaning on my care and protection. I looked round the dreary room; it was changed, it was glorified, I could have shouted with joy. Only now when it had passed from me did I gauge the depth of the shadow of death! Only now did I measure, with a pistol in my hand, my fear of the rope!

True, we were still in peril, but my heart rose to meet the danger, and exulted in it. I knew Levi to be a cur and his men were much of the same kidney. I reckoned that we were hardly two miles from the main road along which our patrols would be constantly passing in the day-time; nor more than four miles as the crow flies, from the detachment at the ferry. A little shooting on Levi's part or ours would soon bring our people about his ears.

Still, we must, for a time, depend on ourselves and our own resources, and we had only one pistol and six cartridges. A second pistol was a thing much to be desired. So while I kept watch at the window, the girl at a word from me fell to ransacking the men's blankets and saddle-bags.

The search proved fruitless, but by the time it had failed, the man had taken my message. We heard an outburst of oaths, and the sound of feet running along the road; a moment and several figures showed phantom-like through the mist. There was a second outbreak of blasphemy, then for a time, silence.

"The rascals are consulting," I said. "That will not raise their courage. Councils of war never fight."

The girl did not answer and I looked at her. She was sitting on a box rocking herself to and fro, her elbows on her knees, her face hidden in her hands. Then I understood. Our defence, our safety, what was passing here, these were small things to her. It was still the news, the news that she craved, the news

252

for which she pined, the news that she coveted, as she rocked herself to and fro in an agony of impatience.

I thrust my head out of the window. "Are you coming?" I shouted.

At that Levi showed himself, timidly and at a distance. "What cursed trick is this?" he shouted. "What'd she reckon to fetch us here for to jockey us in this fashion? Do you hear, if you don't come down, I'll burn the whole house and you in it! S'help me, if I won't!"

"Then you'll burn your horses," I replied. "And bring our detachment from the ferry on you. See? And see this, too, you cowardly rogue. Give up the messenger you've seized! Give him up! Or we'll raise such a racket as shall bring my people on you quickly! We have your horses, and you cannot recover them without coming under fire."

This was true for we had found two knot-holes in the floor, that commanded the stable below. I fancied that this would go some way towards bringing them to terms, for I knew that in the eyes of such men as these their horses ranked after their own skins.

Levi was silent a moment, digesting the information. Then, "What is all this?" he asked plaintively. "What messenger d'you want? We've none of your messengers."

"The messenger is Tom, Captain Wilmer's negro," I answered. "We know that you've seized him. It's no use lying to us."

"I'll come up and talk," he said.

"No, you won't!" I replied, scenting a trap. "If you come too close I'll put a bullet through you. I'll give you five minutes to decide. Move off!"

He drew off sullenly, and disappeared round the corner of the house.

The girl still rocked herself to and fro, and after a moment of thought I left the window — at some risk — and touched her on the shoulder. "If it were bad news," I said, "they would not have kept it from you."

She looked up at me, a light in her eyes. "Say it again," she said.

I repeated it. "If I could believe that!" she cried, and clapped her hands to her face.

"I can see no other meaning in it," I argued. "If he brought bad news, would he come so early?"

She stood up. "I must know!" she cried passionately. "I must know! I will go down! I will make them tell me! I will wring it from them! Am I to hide here while they know all?" And falling impetuously upon the litter which we had piled upon the trap-door she dragged away the uppermost case, heavy as it was, before I could hinder her. She seized the next, and strove to move it.

I was between two fires. I had left the window unguarded, and I could not tell what was passing outside. On the other hand I could not let her go down and place herself in the power of these miscreants, who, unless they were fools, would hold her as a hostage for my surrender. I caught her by the arm. "Don't!" I cried. "You are mad!"

But she would not listen, she persisted. She struggled with me, and I had only one arm. I had to use my full strength. I dragged her away at last, and in the excitement, having the unguarded window on my mind and the fear of what the men might do while she kept me thus, I shook her — I shook her angrily.

"Come back to your senses!" I said. "I am not going to let you do it! Do you hear! You are not going down!"

"I must!" she cried, struggling with me.

"You will not!" I said.

She ceased to struggle at that, and appeared to come to herself. Then — I still held her firmly by the arm — a blush dyed her face to the roots of her hair. Her eyes fell. "Let me go," she muttered.

"Will you do as I say?" I cried. "Will you be guided?"

"Yes," she said, her lips quivering. There were tears in her eyes.

"And give up this mad idea?"

"Yes."

"That is better," I replied. "Then put that case back, if you please. The news will be neither better nor worse because you do not hear it." And I let her go, and turned quickly to the window, intent, as far as appearances went, upon Levi and the gang.

But if there had been anything to note, if Levi had made a move at that moment, I doubt if I should have seen it. The contest had not taken two minutes, but it had changed all our relations. The struggle and her surrender, the contact between us — our hands had hardly met hitherto — had put the spark to a train that in my case was already laid. My blood was in a tumult, my face as hot as hers, my heart beat furiously. What her feelings were I could only guess. But the tell-tale blood that had waved its signal in her cheek, her sudden confusion, her drooping head, if these did no more than own the man's mastery, they were such an advance on anything that had passed between us that it was no wonder that I forgot the peril, Levi, the rogues, all.

A minute or two, during which I dared not look at her, brought me to my senses. I saw that the

256

mist was thinner, that the sun was beginning to peer through it. Soon we should be able to look abroad, and Levi and his men, surprised in the open and almost within view of the highway, might find the boot on the other leg. My spirits rose; and again I remembered, and they sank as quickly. The news! The news that she longed for so hungrily, from which she expected so much. How could it be good? I knew Rawdon too well, and the story of poor André was too fresh in my memory. Besides, the mens' ultimatum could hardly have been delivered And were the news bad, as bad it must be, it mattered little what she felt for me now. The feeling would not survive the shock.

I stole a glance at her, She was listening. Presently her eyes came to meet mine. "Surely," she urged, "the five minutes are past."

"Yes," I said, "they must be." And looking warily out of the window I shouted.

No one answered, no one appeared. But while I hung over the sill and waited sounds that I did not understand came to my ears, vaguely at first, but presently more clearly. It seemed to me that a struggle was going on not far off. "I believe Tom has got away!" I exclaimed. "Or they are fighting among themselves. Listen!"

The report of a gun startled us. The girl sprang

to the window and breathless, trembling with anxiety she leant far out; so far that I drew her back.
"Have a care!" I said. "They might take you for
me!" Then, "Who is this?" I asked.

A man had appeared at a little distance from us,
and was approaching the door. I knew at a glance
that it was not Levi; Levi would have hailed me
from a distance or sneaked up under cover. This
man came forward without fear, a little switch
in his hand. "It's not Tom!" I said. The mist
blurred the man's outline.

"Tom? No!" she answered looking at me
piteously. Then, "Ask him! He knows! He
—" She could not finish. She clung to me. It
was only later that I took in the full wonder and
the meaning of this. She clung to me, though the
news bad or good, was not known to her.

"Halloa!" I shouted to the man who was still a
few yards from the door but was coming on as coolly
as if he were approaching his own house. "Is it
good news?" I had no doubt of the answer but it
was best to know the worst, best to have it over.

He looked up and saw me. He nodded. "Yes,
it's good!" he said. Then he nodded again. "Quite
good, Major."

I stared confounded, while she — for a moment
her weight hung heavy on my arm. Then she sighed,

stiffened herself, and drew away from me. I did not look at her. For one thing I dared not, and for another, what if the news were not true? Who was this man, and what did he know?

"Is she there?" he asked, looking up and tapping his neat boot with his switch.

"Yes," I said, still doubting.

"Well, send her down, will you?" he replied. "There's somebody waiting for her at the back of the mill."

Then I knew the man. It was Marion — General Marion, for he had been raised to that rank since I had parted from him.

CHAPTER XIII

CONSTANTIA AT SARATOGA

"We don't think much of Miss X — Y — my dear,
Quite too fond of the British Officers."
LIFE OF ELIZA PINCKNEY.

The girl's wits were so much more nimble than mine that she had staggered under the news, recovered herself and done much to remove the boxes from the trap-door before I could turn to help her. Then it hurt me a little, I confess, that she had not a look for me, or a word. All her thoughts were with Marion. She flew to the ladder, descended it, and vanished, as if I had not existed, or as if I had not for twenty-four hours spent myself in the effort to undo the misfortune which I had brought upon her!

It was foolish of me to feel this, and more foolish to resent it. But I did both and that so keenly, that I was in no haste to descend. The news was good, her father was safe, and that was enough for her. That was all for which she cared. Why should I go down among them, whoever they were! There are times when we are all children, and stand aloof in sullenness, saying that we will not play.

True, I had not done much for her — she had played her own game, it seemed. But I had done what I could.

So it was Marion who presently, cool and neat and smoking the eternal cigar, climbed up to me. He took in the wretched room with an appreciative eye. "Home of the patriot!" he said, smiling. "This is what you drive us to, Major."

"It's as full of fleas," I cried peevishly, "as a starving dog!"

"I know," he said. "The Carolina flea is grand. But I suppose that you've not heard the news? We've hoodwinked you again, Craven." This time his tone was more grave but his eyes still twinkled. "Wilmer walked past your sentries at nine o'clock last night, and he's not a hundred miles away at this moment and as free as air."

"Thank God!" I said. And I meant it.

"Yes, you can't fight a people, Major," he continued. "You can't fight a people. You may be what you like on your side of the big water, but here you're no more than a garrison! You're like a blind man plunging hither and thither among people who see!"

"Suppose you descend to particulars," I said coldly.

"The particular is Con, God bless her!" he

answered. "There's an American girl for you! There's a girl of spirit! Pity," he continued demurely, "that she's a rebel! She wasn't blind. By heaven, there wasn't a stone she left unturned from the moment you left the Bluff! She sent to me and drew me into her plans. She sent to Levi, and drew him in — silly girl — as if any good could come of those rogues! She drew you into the scheme and made use, good use of you, Major. But all the time she was her own best friend. She won a twenty-four hours respite from your commander — that was life or death to her. Then, after learning through her nigger and others the ways of the place, she cast dust in your folks' eyes by riding away to appeal to Cornwallis — it was uncommonly clever that! And there, I give your folks credit — you can play the gentleman when you please, Major. If all of you played it and played it always," he went on with a smile, "things would be very different south of the Dan River. I should not be web-footed with living in the swamps of the Pee Dee; and Sumter —" his smile broadened — "would not be sore with riding bare-backed horses in his shirt."

"I'm glad that you think we behaved well," I said dryly. "But the fact does not explain Captain Wilmer's escape."

"No, but Con made her market of the fact, God

bless her, as of other things," he answered. And he looked at me so meaningly that the color rose in my face. "She used it to get her interview with her father, and — of course you were too gentlemanly to search her."

"Which means?"

"That she took in a nigger outfit, and the rest of it, under her skirts — wig, stain, and all. That night her boy, Tom, took the place of the tavern waiter and carried in Wilmer's supper and stayed while he ate it. At nine o'clock there was a fight among some negro teamsters in front of the tavern, and under cover of the skirmish Wilmer carried out the tray, with a napkin in his mouth, crossed to the tavern, walked up the yard as bold as brass, and vanished. Clever wasn't it? Ten minutes later when the guard was changed his black walked out too, carrying the plates. I suppose, first and last," Marion continued, thoughtfully tapping his boot, "a dozen persons white and black, knew of the plan before it came off — knew where the 'possum was — and not one peached. Weigh that, Major, weigh that, if you please, and tell me, if you can, that you still think you will beat us! Why you're beaten already!"

"But Tom —"

"Oh, the nigger ran his risk," Marion replied

carelessly. "Wasn't he Wilmer's boy, born on the place? He'd do that and more. And after all he got clear. And by God — I don't think that I ever saw a more curious thing· than I saw just now, and I'll wager something it's a sight that I shall never see again."

"What was it?" I asked dully. Seven words he had said earlier "she made use, good use of you" were repeating themselves over and over again in my brain.

"What was it? Why, a white woman on her knees kissing a black man's hands! A spoiled nigger, Major! You may take it from me, a spoiled nigger! Wilmer may as well free him. He'll never be worth a continental cent to him again."

"It was a clever plan," I said. But I could not throw much spirit into my words.

"Oh, she's a jewel is Madam Constantia!" he answered. "It makes me laugh now to think how she made use of us all. She wanted me to beat up Winnsboro' at sunrise to-day if Tom's plan failed; as if I were likely to venture my fellows against the whole British army! No, I couldn't do that, even for Wilmer. But I told her I would move up to Camden and be at hand at daybreak to-day in case he was followed; and that if possible I'd fall back by this road. As a fact Tom was here first with the news, but those rogues — there's a woman's weak point, she don't know whom to trust — seized him, poor devil, for some reason of their own and when we landed we found him tied up in a shed at the back."

"What's become of Levi?" I asked. Not that I cared one way or the other. She had made use of me, good use of me — with the rest!

"Gone!" he said curtly. "And wise to go! We shall take their horses. That'll be some punishment. I would have strung him up with good will, but there are times when we need a dirty tool."

"Though you prefer a clean one," I said bitterly. And I thought of myself.

He laughed. "Madam Con will in future," he said. "She's had a lesson. But, lord, how happy that girl is! Her father is safe, and she has saved him!"

"Well, he's no use as a spy any more!" I said. I was feeling mad, as the saying is.

"That's true," he replied, not losing his good humor for a moment. "As an American André — by your leave, Major — he's blown upon. The risk always made the girl miserable, and many's the night I, fancy, that she has not slept for thinking of him. Now that is at an end, and she's doubly happy. But there," breaking off, "let us go into the open air. In a few minutes I must be moving. My men are on the other bank, and when the fog lifts we are too near your post at the Ferry and too far from our own supports to be comfortable. I've a boat behind the mill and I can cross in five minutes, but I shall not be happy until we are on the other side of the Black River. I would not have come so far for any one but that girl."

"Nor I," I said, forgetting myself for a moment. Fortunately he had his back to me and perhaps he did not hear. A moment later we were outside. "I am told that Rawdon has ordered you to be put under arrest," he said.

"You heard that?"

"Oh, we hear everything. The blind man's moves are easy to follow. For the matter of that Con saw your sword on my lord's table. He was polite as pie to her," he continued, with a chuckle. "He was another of them! He said a good deal about you; said that you'd thrown your commission in his face, and he didn't wonder — I suppose that was a compliment to her — but that discipline must be maintained, and he didn't know but that he'd have to send you home."

"There are times when we are all fools," I said gloomily.

"Suppose I make you a prisoner?" he suggested.

"You would be a mean cur, General Marion, if you did!" I cried. For the moment I was alarmed. Then I saw that he was smiling.

"Peppery as that are you?" he said. "I don't wonder that my lord was for putting you under arrest. But don't be afraid. You've set us a good example and we are going to follow it. Your fault, Major, is that you think you are the only gentlemen in the world. Whereas we are of the same blood or better!" He drew himself up, a heroic little figure, not untouched by vanity. "Of the same blood or better!" he repeated. "And if there are no gentlemen south of the Potomac River, then believe me, sir, there are no gentlemen anywhere in the world."

"Granted," I said cordially. "But the misfortune is that you are not all of a pattern."

"No, nor you," he riposted sharply. "There are good and bad, fine and mean in every country, sir, and some day we shall understand that, and shall cease to set down the faults of the few to the account of the many. War is tolerable, Major; war between you and me! It is the abuse of war that is intolerable. But I must go, or may be you will be making me a prisoner. My compliments to Tarleton when you see him — a good man but over sharp; over sharp, Major! Tell him that the Swamp Fox will give him many a run yet, and will not be the first to go to ground if I can help it."

We had walked a little way from the mill, and while we talked a couple of men had led out the horses. I had a glimpse of them as they vanished round the corner of the build.ng. Marion held out his hand.

"If we meet again, Major," he said, "we will shoot at one another in all good fellowship — all soldiers of the right sort are comrades in arms. Meantime I wish you good-fortune. And if, when the war s over — I expect that by that time you will be once more a prisoner on parole — you have a fancy for a little duck-shooting, there is none better than on the Marion Plantation in St. John's Parish."

I could not resist his good humor and, depressed as I was, I returned his grasp with spirit. It was impossible not to admire what I had heard of him. and equally impossible not to like what I had seen of him. There was in him a sparkle and a gaiety as well as an indomitable spirit that explained the hold he had over his men, a hold that was firmest in the darkest days and when the Swamp Fox's life was not more easy than his. "Certainly," I said, "I will remember the duck-shooting, General. And if I can procure leave for you to reside on your plantation, of which I have no doubt we shall still be in possession, we may have the pleasure of shooting the ducks in company."

"Bah!" he cried laughing. "Long live the Thirteen States!"

"Long live King George!" I answered. "A clement and —"

"A very stupid sovereign!" he retorted gaily. He waved his hat, and I waved mine. I understood that he did not wish me to learn the strength of his party, or who were with him; and I made no attempt to follow him. The sun was shining through the mist as he went round the house and disappeared in the direction of the river.

Alas, the passing gaiety with which his good temper had infected me went with him. For days I had lived upon excitement. The exhilaration of movement, of effort, of danger, had borne me on. Above all the presence of the girl, whose nearness set my pulses bounding, had filled my thoughts and buoyed me up. Now in a twinkling I stood stripped of all, and shivering. Excitement, exhilaration, danger, Constantia, all were gone and I stood alone, by this cursed morass. I faced a future as flat and dreary as the prospect before my eyes; and in the rebound, I could almost have found it in my heart to pitch myself into one of the pale channels which

the sunlight revealed running this way and that
across the moss. The gaunt house beside me was
not more lonely than I felt; and ungrateful as we
too often are to Providence — before whom I bow
in reverence as I write — the thought that I had
just escaped from a violent death went for little in
my thoughts.

I was digging a hole in the mud with my heel
and thinking of this when I heard footsteps behind
me. I turned sharply; who can measure the swift-
ness with which hope leaps up in the heart? But
the steps were only Marion's. He had appeared
again at the corner of the house.

He did not approach me but called to me from a
distance. "Have you any message for my god-
daughter," he asked, "before I go?"

She has sent him back, I thought, to cover her
retreat. Something, she feels, is due to me; and
this kind of left-handed message saves her face. I
felt it, I felt it sorely, but I pulled myself together —
was I to remind her of her debt? "To be sure," I
said as cooly as I could. "Be good enough to
congratulate her. Say how glad I am to have been
of use to her — along with others."

"I'll 'tell her," he called out. "Very good!"
And he laughed. "Good-bye, then, till better
times. And don't forget the duck-shooting!"

I made him some reply. He waved his hat. He disappeared.

So it was all over. That was all that she had to say to me.

For a little while, for a few minutes, anger warmed me. Then that, too, died down and left me chilled and miserable. I ground my heel farther into the mud. The water welled up and mechanically I went on working at, and enlarging, the hole.

I was paying dearly for a few hours of happiness; very dearly for the belief which had lasted no more than a few hours, that she loved me. I wondered now on what I had founded it. On the fact that she had drawn back when it had come to hazarding my life? On that moment when she had turned to me for help? On that other when she had clung to me? On a blush, a look? Oh, fool! These were nothings, I saw now; things imponderable, intangible, evasive as the air, fugitive as the wind. She had not loved me. She had only made her market of me. She had only made use of me. She had drawn me into her plans with others, with Tom, with Levi, with her god-father, with Rawdon, with Paton! She had made her market of us all — and saved her father's life.

Well, I was glad she had! I would not for the world have had it otherwise. If my love for her

271

held anything that was good and honest and un-
selfish — and I thought it did — I must rejoice with
her, and I would. She owed me nothing, while
I owed her father my life. And so at worst we
were quits.

By this time the sun had drunk up the last of the
fog, and showed the flats in all their ugliness. Well,
I would be going. There was no more to be done
here. It was all over.

I went into the mill and stood staring at the troop-
horses. I saw that with only one arm I should find
it no easy matter to saddle them, but it had to be
done. First, however, I went upstairs to get my
cloak, and I found not mine only — on a box beside
the expiring fire lay hers. So she had left it as
lightly as she had left me! Beside it, cast heed-
lessly on the floor lay the pistol that had done so
much for us. She had not given a second thought
to that either. I took it, and hid it in my breast.
It had lain in hers when she had been unhappy,
when the heart, against which it had pressed, had
throbbed to bursting with the pain of fear and of
suspense. I would never part with it.

I went down, carrying the cloaks, and began to
deal with the horses. With some difficulty I saddled
and bridled the one I had ridden, but the gray
proved to be a rogue. As often as I forced the bit

between its teeth it flung up its head and got rid of it before I could secure the cheekstrap. Thrice I tried and thrice the brute baffled me and once hit me heavily on the chin. A fourth time I tried and failing gave over with an oath, and laid my face against the saddle. It was her saddle, and heaven knows whether it was that which overcame me, or my helplessness, or the feeling that they had left me to do this, but —

"You must let me help you with that."

I started. The rush of joy was so over-powering, the shock of hearing her voice so unexpected, that it dazzled me as if a flame had passed before my eyes. On that instant of rapture followed another — of un-reasoning and unreasonable shame. How long had she been there? What had she seen — she who had once called me a milksop? "I was tightening a girth," I mumbled, keeping my head lowered.

"Yes," she said, "but it has slipped again, I think."

I groped for it — it was indeed hanging under the horse's barrel. I murmured that the stable was so dark that it was almost impossible —

"You must let me help you."

"You shall in a moment," I answered. "I will just fix this." And then — "I thought that you had gone," I muttered.

"Gone?" she cried.

"With General Marion."

"Gone without thanking you?" she exclaimed. "Oh, impossible! You could not think that of me! Gone without —"

"It was some mistake," I said.

"It was a very great mistake," she answered. "Will you allow me to pass you?"

I made way for her to pass to the horse's head. The stable was dark, I have said, but as she went by, something prompted her to turn, and look me in the face. "The brute hit me on the chin," I said hurriedly.

She did not speak. I pulled down the gray's head, and she thrust the bit between its teeth. Then she proceeded to fasten the cheekstrap, but she was so long about it that I saw that her fingers were trembling and that her breath came as short and quick as if she had been running. "My fingers are all thumbs this morning," she said with a queer laugh. "With joy, I suppose. But there, it's done, Major Craven. Now I must get my cloak," she added, and she slipped quickly by me as if she were in a hurry.

"I have it," I said.

"And my pistol?"

"I have that too," I said.

"Then I suppose that we had better be going," she answered. "But perhaps I ought to explain," she continued, as she stood in the doorway with her back to the light. "General Marion could not take me with him. He is making for the Pee Dee and the great marshes, and hopes to be on the other side of Lynch's creek by night. He took Tom but he said that I should embarrass him."

"I see."

"He thought that you would perhaps escort me as far as Camden," she continued soberly. "I have friends there who will receive me for the night and send me home to-morrow by Rocky Mount and the fords of the Catawba. He fancied that I had better avoid Winnsboro'."

"I agree with him," I said.

"I might be arrested, he fancied?"

"It is not impossible," I assented dryly. I felt that something was closing in on me and stopping all the sources of speech. This ordered plan, this business-like arrangement — I was to be of use to the end it seemed. Just of use! I strove desperately to resist the thought and yet I could not.

"Then if there is nothing else," she said slowly, "we might — be going, I suppose?"

"I suppose so," I answered heavily. And I turned the horses round.

"Or — do you think," she suggested uncertainly, "that we had better eat something before we start?"

"Let us eat it outside, then!" I replied. "I cannot breathe in this place."

"Yet you were ready enough to enter it!" she retorted. And then before I could answer, "I must see what they've left!" she exclaimed. "There must be something up-stairs."

She went nimbly up the ladder, leaving me staring after her. I turned the horses round and secured them. Then, in a brown study, I went out and for the first time I passed round the building, and saw the wide river gliding by, and beyond it across the marshes the long low ridge that goes by the name of the High Hills of Santee. The sun was shining on the distant ridge, and on the water, and compared with the prospect from the other side of the mill the view was cheerful and even gay. I spread her cloak on a pile of lumber that littered the wharf, and then I went back to fetch her.

She had found some corn-bread and molasses, and some cold cooked rice. Even with the help of whisky of which there was more than of anything else, it was a poor feast and she spread it in silence while I looked on — thinking and thinking. From here to Camden was so many hours, two or three or four. So long I should have her company. Then we should part. As I rode away I should look back and see her framed in a doorway; or I should stand myself and see her grow small as she receded, until she turned some corner and was gone. And I should know that this was the end. So many hours, two or three or four! And heavy on me all the time the knowledge that I should spoil them by my unhappy temper, or my dullness, or that strange feeling that benumbed my tongue and took from me the power of speech.

She looked up. "It is quite ready," she said. And then, lowering her tone to a whisper, "Let us remember the last time we ate," she said reverently, "and be thankful."

"Amen," I said. "I thank God for your sake."

"And I thank too," she answered in a voice that shook a little, "all who helped me."

"Tom?"

"Ah, dear brave Tom!" she cried, tears in her voice.

We were eating by this time, and to lighten the talk, "I am not sure," I said, "that General Marion approved of the manner in which you thanked him."

"Thanked Tom? Because I kissed his hand? I believe I did," she added ingenuously. "Oh, it was a small thing! Surely it was a small thing to do for him who had risked his life for me!"

Our eyes met. For a moment the red flamed in her cheeks but she met my look bravely. "I am not ashamed," she said. "I would do the same again in the same case."

The eyes that fell were mine. I was tongue-tied. Here was an opening but how could I say that I was in the same case. How could I claim that the risk I had run was to be compared with that which Tom had run. Or how could I claim at all as a debt — what I wanted. Perish the thought! So I went on eating, silent and stupid, thinking of the few, few hours that separated us from Camden, thinking of the long, long time that would follow. She said one or two things disjointedly; that her father would free Tom, of course; that he was a very clever negro, and wonderful as a bone-setter.

"I should know that," I said.

"Yes," she assented; and I stole a glance at her. She had found means to plait up her hair and arrange her dress. She was another creature now from the desperate, driven, tragical girl who had clung to me that morning, whose heart had beaten for an instant against mine, whose pistol at this moment lay hard and cold on my breast. My courage sank lower and lower. Of that girl I had had hopes, on her I had had a claim. But this one was a stranger.

Presently we had finished, and she rose and went down to the river to wash her hands.

When she had done this she turned and came up the bank again, swinging her hat in her hand, and softly crooning some song of praise. The sun flamed from the water behind her, and out of that light she came towards me, tall and slender and gracious, and with such a glory of thanksgiving in her face, that my pride, or whatever it was, that stood between her and me, and kept me silent, gave way and broke! What matter what she thought? What matter if she trod me under foot, held me cheap, disdained me? What matter? I went to meet her.

"You did that for Tom," I said. "Have you nothing for me? For me, too?"

Her grave eyes met mine. She was nearly of a height with me. "For you," she said, "I have all that you choose to ask."

"Yourself?" I cried.

"If it be your pleasure."

And that, it may be thought, should have satisfied me, who an instant before had despaired. But so presumptuous is success I was already jealous, already exigent. "Ah, not as a debt?" I cried. "If you cannot give me your love, Con?"

"I cannot," she answered with smiling eyes. "It

has been given to you this month past." Then as she hung back from me, blushing divinely, "They have touched Tom's black hands," she said.

"God bless them for it!" I answered.

Later she told me that she had loved me from the hour I had kept silence as to her part in the outrage at the Bluff. "I was ashamed, oh, I was horribly ashamed of it," she said. "I knew that neither my father nor my god-father would have done that! Yet, I am not sure that it was not earlier than that? I think it was your mention of the soldier's wife when you were yourself in — in danger — that clung to my memory, and would not be shaken off, and —"

"Poor Simms!" I said. "And I once envied him!"

．　．　．　．　．　．　．　．　．　．

At Camden the Wateree becomes the Catawba, and happiness becomes memory or anticipation, according as you gaze up or down the stream. For there, in a tiny parlor in a white frame house looking on a poplar wood, I parted from Constantia, and left her with the friends who were to see her as far as Rocky Mount on her homeward journey. I fear 'that they were rebels. But there are things which it is wise to leave *sub silentio ;* the dog that has found a bone does not bark. And my position was delicate.

I felt that position grow more delicate in proportion as, with my face turned towards Winnsboro', I approached the camp. I was not sad; the future held that which would make amends for present evils. But I knew that I had an unpleasant passage before me, and my conscience was not quite clear. At any rate I had misgivings, and taking care to reach the camp at sunset, and as the guard was changing, I made my way to Paton's quarters without beat of drum. I was lucky enough to find him before the Provost-Marshal found me.

He shook with laughter when he saw me. "Upon my honor, Major," he said. "We are all vastly obliged to you! You are a whole company of players in yourself. As the hero-errant who relieves the Distressed Damsel and releases the Beleaguered Knight you fill the stage. The camp is agog with you. The latest about you is that the rebels have hung you from the roof of a remote house in the marshes. And, lo, we are all lamenting you, when in you walk as coolly as if the Dragon at Headquarters, robbed of his prey, were not breathing Court Martials and Firing Parties and the worst threats against you."

"I had nothing to do with it," I said stoutly.

"Innocent!"

"That is what I am."

"Well, you will have to persuade my lord of it," he retorted. "And you'll find your work prepared for you! Francis Rawdon-Hastings is in no mean rage, my lad. The sooner you placate him the better. I hope the lady has come to give evidence for you?"

I pooh-poohed this, but I took his hint and I went straight to Headquarters, leaving him mightily amused. There, the storm was not slow to break over me. My conduct was disgraceful, contumacious, subversive of all discipline, flat mutiny. I had taken advantage of my position and his lordship's friendship, and the rest. I had collogued with convicted rebels, I had wandered over the country with suspected persons. I should be tried by Court Martial, I should find, whoever I was, that I could not do these things with impunity! D — d if I could!

When I could be heard — and Webster, generally kind and easy-going, was almost as bad as the Irishman, "But, my lord," I said, "What had I to do with the escape? It was not I who permitted the lady to visit her father?"

That hit them between wind and water. They stared. "Then it was she?" my lord exclaimed.

"Who took in the disguise, my lord? As I have since learned — it was. And I venture to say that there is not an officer in the service in your lordship's position, or in any other, who would punish a daughter for the attempt to save her father's life!"

"The devil is that she did save it, sir!" he answered with vexation. But he could not regain his old fluency, and presently he asked me to tell him all I knew. I did so, feeling sure that he would be unable to withhold his admiration; and the final result as far as I was concerned was a reprimand and ten days confinement to camp — and an intolerable amount of jesting! Some wag, Paton, I am afraid, discovered that her name was Constantia and adding it to our Osgodby motto, the single word "Virtus," scrawled a whole series of " Virtus et Constantia" over my books and papers. Perhaps in a silly way I liked it.

Certainly this was the least of my troubles. The greatest, or at any rate, that which tried me most sharply, was the fact that I could not communicate with Constantia without laying myself open to suspicion. For several months I received no news of her and had to content myself with doing all that I could to procure the release of her brother. Of me, indeed, she heard through the mysterious channels which were open to her side. But she was too thoughtful of me and too careful of my honor to approach me through them. At length there came a change laden with bitter sorrow to her. Her father fell in the engagement at Guildford Court House in a gallant but vain attempt to stem the flight of the Northern Militia. Stricken to the heart — though she had the satisfaction of knowing that he had fallen on the field of honor — she abandoned the Bluff which, exposed to incursions from both sides, was no longer a safe place for her, With Aunt Lyddy and Mammy Jacks she came down to Charles Town.

For how much the desire to see me counted in inducing her to take this step, she knew and I guessed. And fortune which had frowned, presently smiled on us. I was attached to General Leslie's force in Charles Town, and there I saw her almost daily and learned to know her as I had learned to love her. I passed unscathed through the fight at Eutaw Springs: she uninjured through many months of devoted attendance on her sick and wounded countrymen. A month before the evacuation of the city by the British, and when the approach of peace had already softened men's minds and made things easy which had been hard before, we were married at St. Philip's.

We passed our honeymoon on the Marion Plantation in St. John's Parish with a pass granted by General Greene; and there Constantia's brother, whose freedom I had procured two months before, joined us. When he, with Aunt Lyddy and Mammy Jacks, went north to take up again the threads of life at the Bluff, we crossed to the islands and thence sailed for Europe in the Falmouth Packet.

With all our love for one another the last night in harbor was a sad night for both. For Constantia, because she was leaving her native land. For me it was saddened by the sight of the ships that lay beside us, laden with those who had supported our cause and must now, for other reasons than Constantia's, face a life of exile. My heart bled for them; nay, as I write twenty years later, it is still sore for them. But the wound is healing, if slowly, and I look forward in hope and with confidence to a day when the birth and the traditions which we share will once more unite the two branches of our race, it may be in a common cause, it may be in the face of a common peril.

So may it be!

Lightning Source UK Ltd.
Milton Keynes UK
UKHW011950060219
336834UK00010B/615/P